Loyalty and Envy

Loyalty and Envy

Revenge For My Mother

JeDonna Mathis
   Santana Global Publications

Loyalty and Envy

Revenge For My Mother

Written By: JeDonna Mathis

Where My Pen Leaks Fire LLC

thewriterjm89@gmail.com

Copyright © 2022 JeDonna Mathis

Notice of Copyright

All rights reserved under International Copyright Law. Except as permitted under the U.S. Copyright Act of 1976, no part of this publication may be reproduced, distributed, or transmitted in any form or by any means, or stored in a database or retrieval system, without the prior written permission of the publisher.

Where My Pen Leaks Fire LLC

Front Cover Art: Navi Robins

nsgraphicstudio.com

Editing by: Santana Global Publications

Publishing Company: Santana Global Publications

For information contact:

theservicedesk@santanaglobal.com

www.santanaglobal.com

First Printing Edition, 2022

Printed in: The United States, First Edition

Contents

Acknowledgements — ix

Part I.

1. Gotta Go Back Home — 1
2. Break It Down — 8
3. Don't Play With The Game — 29
4. A Long Time Coming — 33
5. Time to turn it up a Notch — 44
6. Tell Me Something Man — 51
7. You Done Fucked Up — 68
8. Make Him Sweat A little Bit — 85
9. Let's Talk Sis — 96
10. Pick A Side And Pick It Now (QC) — 105
11. It's On Now — 107
12. Tie His Ass Up Spooks — 119
13. Y'all Need To know (Envy) — 122
14. The Plot Thickens — 141

About the Author	153
Special Thanks	155
Special Thanks	156

Acknowledgements

I want to take the time to acknowledge all my readers. I appreciate all of you for your support. For those who took the time to read my stories, listen to me read my stories, and those who offered feedback while I worked on my rough draft. I would also like to acknowledge my sis Ty Brown for never hesitating to listen and offer feedback and read my manuscripts and pushing me when I was ready to give up. Thank you so much! I want to acknowledge Author Navi Robins for his great work on the cover.

I.

Gotta Go Back Home

Sitting here reflecting on the words my mom said to me before she passed away.

"Take care of you and your sister, no matter what. You girls only have each other. Trust *no one* else, you hear me, Loyalty?"

Her voice replayed over and over in my head daily. Tears began to roll down my cheeks as I thought about her. I felt like I had let her down. From the sound of it, my sister was getting out of control. Baby sis was definitely a wildcard. I'd find out firsthand exactly how and fix this.

My mother named us Loyalty and Envy. We lived in Grand Rapids, Michigan. My mother told us she gave us those names because she got pregnant in the streets. She always said that loyalty and envy were the two main things in life that could either make you or break you. We were two years apart. I was twenty-two and she was twenty.

Our momma was not your average mother. She was a very well-known drug dealer. Some would say she was a Queen Pen for sure. She went by the name Lady J. I don't think no one even knew her real name but us. Growing up, I've watched my mother sack dope and count money daily. I watched it so much that I could count money in my sleep front to back. It seemed as if she never slept. She was a straight night owl. Her bedroom didn't even have a bed in it if I recall. The sight of it was shocking, especially because of the layout of the rest of the house. She called her room 'the workshop'. There was nothing but a glass dining room table, a futon, camera monitors, a tv, and a big ass safe. She hid her safe under the floor in the bottom of the closet. It was a black, steel, shiny box. No one knew that it was there, other than the members of the household. I mean our house was plushed out completely from top to bottom, except for our mother's room.

During our childhood, we always had two houses. Being young, I didn't know that house number two was the trap house. Well, at least not until I got a little older and put two and two together. My momma didn't trust anyone to babysit us other than this older lady named Ms. June. Ms. June took my mother in a few times when she ran away from foster care. She really loved Ms. June. She passed away a year before my mother. We were always with her or at home most of the time.

Momma would say, "It's best for them if y'all stayed at home, I would kill the city if something happened to y'all."

Momma was very protective over my sister and I. She was strict but understanding with us. My mother was crazy as hell, too. When I was younger, I noticed that the people who stayed here never came to our other home, either. No one, and I mean no one was allowed there without my mom's permission.

My little sister Envy acts just like our mom in many ways. The streets are Envy's sanctuary. Everything about the streets gave her an undeniable thrill. Our mother left us set with everything, including her spot in the game, which came with a lot of money and respect in the streets. There was also a lot of heat, thanks to my sister, so I heard. I guess she had a heated feud going on with someone, and it was causing a paper shortage. That girl kept me worried, I know that much.

When I was ten years old, I should have been playing with Barbies and lip gloss. Instead, I was busy learning how to properly load and unload a 9mm. Not too long after that, I knew how to take a whole gun apart and put it back together in a quick time frame. After a while, I became fascinated with guns of all kinds.

I told my mother I wanted to go to college and her response was a life lesson.

"Baby, college won't teach you survival," she said as she stared me in the eyes.

Someone really fucked her up as a child. She grew up in multiple foster homes. My mom was very cutthroat and bold. She didn't hold you up one bit. It was hard to joke with a very serious person. She just didn't give a fuck about nothing but us, herself, and money.

Once she made us watch her cut a man's tongue out. She did it because he took a detective's card. His actions convinced my mom that he was not to be. I was so scared, but my crazy ass sister Envy found it intriguing.

Once my mom got back in the car, she said, "If he takes the card, he'll take the stand. This game is to be sold, never told."

We never saw that man again. I'm pretty sure she killed him or had someone else do it. People feared her, and they knew crossing her meant death. The crazy part is she did the majority of the killing. She was very open with my sister and I. If Momma had to visit you, the only thing that could possibly save you was money.

Unfortunately, one day someone grew the heart of a lion and killed our mother. I was a junior in high school. My mind was blown. Who would do that? We still haven't found out who did it or why. That truly bothers me, and Lord have mercy on my soul if I ever found out. After my mother passed, I decided to graduate and go off to college. She left us more than enough money. One of her insurance policies paid for my tuition alone. I was going for my Masters in Business, that way I can clean up all this money coming in. Momma definitely kept me studying business, numbers, and marketing at a young age. I was accepted to MSU after graduating top of my senior class. Envy chose to stay home and run with momma's old gang keeping her name alive. She loved every bit of it too. I was so tired of that shit especially after it took our mother away. Don't get me wrong, after my mother was killed, I hustled and hit a few licks sometimes. The streets just didn't really please me. The streets took my mother from us and broke my heart. The streets loved no one, I just wanted more and to get away from all I have seen. So that's when I made the decision to apply and go off to college. By the time I was nineteen turning twenty I was gone.

Look at me now, a year away from graduating with my MBAs and here I am headed back into the streets. I was told that my sister is getting so reckless. I couldn't just let her throw momma's legacy away or get hurt. Just sitting in my car thinking, as I waited on my slow ass sister. Waiting on her to come out of the house to the address she gave me.

Slowly but surely here she comes, trailing behind some fool. "Hey sis can we land him real quick by his crib", she asked? "Come on E", I rolled my eyes. Once they had gotten in and I pulled off. She began to light her blunt up, as she motioned me to make a right onto Eastern from 52nd street. "Now you know you are not smoking in here", I interrupted. "Man, chill sis it's only weed Loyalty", she smirks, lighting it anyways. Hardheaded ass lil girl", I mumbled. "You need to hit the shit and calm your nerves", she laughed. Trying to put it up to my lips. "Stop damn", I smacked her hand. "Where is your friend going?", I asked? "Ok damn, he's going to that liquor store on Oakdale and Eastern at the corner". Coughing as she passed the weed to him.

I admired seeing everything as I drove up Eastern. Been

a minute since I've been home. Harry's Corner was still standing strong I see. Envy whooped some girl ass at that store when we were younger. We were hanging with some kids from school, she and one of the girls had words. My sister can throw them hands too. Rolling through here just brings back so many good memories. They put a Wing Heaven on Burton and Eastern. I must get some soon, I thought to myself.

It didn't take my fast, driving ass long before I pulled into the store parking lot. "Thanks for the ride, Ma ", he spoke up while getting out. "Call me tomorrow", she told him. Envy gave him a kiss and he gave her some money before we pulled off. I just stared at her for a minute. It's been some months since I last saw her. Even though we talk every few days on the phone. In person is always better. She drives me crazy but I love the hell out of her crazy ass. We are very close and our bond was unbreakable.

After dropping her friend off I told her I wanted to see the spot. I needed to see firsthand what was going on. "So, Envy who's been having ya back these days?", I asked her? "My homie Spooks", she replied. "Who is Spooks?", I was puzzled. "We just dropped him off", she smiled. "He's watching your back alright", I smirked. "And he watches it very well", she giggled. "Well, I know you remember lil June that stayed down the street from us", she went on explaining. "Lil June was a nerd sis", I told her. "Well, he's damn good with numbers and he's a natural born killer", she smirked. "What", I shockingly said! "Yea after his mother and grandmother died in that accident the savage came out", she went on. Death of a close loved one can really change you into someone you never knew was in you. "Look sis I'm kinda hungry, I had a long night", she smiled. "What do you want to eat then Ms. night owl", I said. "Take me to Eastern Deli, I want a burger", she responded. "Once we're done eating, I'll get you hipped on everything", she implied.

2.

Break It Down

We arrived at momma's old trap house on Griggs and Paris. So many memories hit me at once seeing this place. I haven't been here to this very place since I left for school. Been kinda avoiding it for real. Don't know why I just couldn't phantom being there. This was the main place my mother spent most of her time. We played in this backyard so much. We had a trampoline back there too. So sometimes she would let the neighborhood kids play over with us. Not having my mother here made shit so awkward. Even when I would come into town, I would try to avoid this street shit period. Envy doesn't know I was called home back to Grand Rapids, by our foster uncle QC. He told me he could be facing major problems and needed my help. I wanted to say no so bad I swear. He also explained to me that my sister has been really trigger happy lately. Her ass also has been letting muthafuckahs slide, being short on their tabs due. Knowing damn well momma never took no shorts. We once watched her kidnap kids about her paper being short. I remember she held a lil boy hostage for two weeks until his parents got all the money owed to her. Crazy huh, yea I know right.

Uncle QC has been around us a long time. He wasn't blood but he is like family. Him and my momma met when they were about twelve at a foster home. They ran away and have been in these streets together ever since. He's actually the only person my mom allowed us to get close to growing up. Uncle QC doesn't play with anybody. Word has always been he killed his own daddy in cold blood, just because he was a crackhead. Guess his dad ran off with his dope or he found out he was using his supply or something. I grew up too scared to even ask. He won't slap me shit, I'll tend to my own business. He helped my mom keep us in line at all times. Just can't understand why he wasn't with my mom the night she was killed. He was out of town. They said the night it happened we were waiting on him. He hasn't been right in the head ever since. They were each other's only family till we came about. Now he barely mentions her name. Uncle QC took over her legacy until one of us was old enough to run it. Momma had that in her will. We never really knew our daddy. I don't remember him too much. Word is he was some Cuban she was madly in love with. One day he just disappeared without a trace. He taught my mother everything she knew though. They met at a drug deal they had going on when she first got in the game. They soon fell in love after that. After Envy was born, he told my mother he was married the whole time. I just remember the last time

I saw him my mother was chasing him, busting her 40cal at him. He never came back for us or even tried. I always wondered if she killed him. After her heart mended it was as if he never existed to us. Hell, I was about four when he left. Uncle QC may know more about him.

"Girls I'll be back I have to make a run", he told us with that deep ass voice. "Envy don't you move till I get back", he mugged her while walking out. "Damn E what did you do", I giggled. "What don't I do?", she smirked! Plopping down on the couch counting her money. The house was still the same as momma left it. Just new furniture and a fireplace was added. Kinda gave me chills for real, I could definitely feel her presence. "So y'all never changed anything", I looked around. "Hell, naw and don't you think about it either Loyalty", Envy glanced up. I ignored her lil order, she called herself giving me. "Man, QC tripping his runs takes forever. I got something on the floor", she mumbled. We both busted out laughing. "So, sis I know it's some fine ass college boys at MSU, are you dating", she mentioned. "Yes, it is but I'm just trying to stay focused and graduate", I answered. "You mean to tell me that your ass is still a virgin", she gasped. "Don't worry about me, worry about your lil pussy between your legs", I rolled my eyes. "Sorry hunny ain't nothing little about this kitty", she danced. As soon as I was about to change the subject I was interrupted by a guest.

The door opened and the finest man I had ever seen walked in. His entrance made time stop ya hear me. He had to be about 6 '3, a gold tee, waves bustin hard. His chocolate skin layered in that all white attire instantly got me hot. His cologne filled the air and he smelled so good. "Hey, Envy you saw my hat", he spoke in such a raspy voice. "Boi I am not your hat keeper", she never looked up. "Who the hell is this? You know QC doesn't allow no company at this house", he walked over. Shaking his head as he walked up to us. "Yo ass already in hot water from the other night", he went on. I interrupted the conversation. "My name is Loyalty and who the fuck are you", I stood up. "Envy get ya lil friend", he waved me off.

He turned to walk towards the kitchen. I smirked at my sister and she nodded her head at me. His gun was budging from the back of his pants. So, I decided to show him just who the fuck I was. Walking up to him and snatching the gun from his back. He turned around so fast but I was just a lil quicker. Dropping the clip to the floor and dismantling his entire gun. "Envy come get your GI Joe ass friend", he yelled! "Fool ain't no friendship in this shit I'm her fucking sister", I inputted. "Sister", he said, looking at Envy with betrayal in his eyes. "Yes, my mom and dad had two of us. Matter of fact, she is the oldest, "she told him. Before we could continue talking Uncle QC walked back in.

"Hey y'all did everyone get acquainted", he asked. "Actually, I was waiting to get a proper introduction boss", his sexy ass said. "Well, this is my niece Loyalty she is Envy's older sister", QC told him. "I kinda met GI Jane when she took my gun apart", he mugged me. QC looked back at me and then the gun laying on the ground shaking his head. "Okay so who is he?", I spoke up. "Loyalty, this is Terrence aka Dollah", my uncle said to me. "Y'all will be working together. So, Dollah makes sure you inform her on everything around here", he instructed. "Wait a minute why not me and Envy working together. I don't know this fool", I snapped. "Loyalty, I don't need all the sassing right now. I have something else I want Envy to do", he rubbed his chin. "Envy I want you to do pickups with Tone awhile", he told her. "What, Tone", she yelled back! "Who is Tone", I asked? "He's a dumbass wanna be gangster can't wait to kiss ass", she whispered to me. "Man, why do I have to work with him", she sighed. "Because I fucking said so after the other night you need a lil rest from the strip club", he snapped back at her. "Plus, he trust you E", Dollah spoke up. "Fuck him", she shrugged her shoulders plopping back onto the couch. "I don't want to hear it, Envy. Until you stop letting these fools slide with my money and stop causing havoc with Spook you will be his best friend. Plus, I hear he has been stealing so I need you to watch him very closely", he explained to her. "You will take his ass out when the time is right", he continued talking to Envy. "So, it's been him this whole time for real", she asked. The look in Envy's eyes was fire. She stormed out of the living room onto the porch.

Before I could run after her my uncle stopped me. "Loyalty let her cool off no time for babying her. Put his gun back together and you two get to work, he ordered me. He walked away into the back room. I wasn't really feeling how he was talking to us, but I kept it quiet for now. "Well, you heard the man put my shit back together", Dollah laughed. I grabbed my purse and my keys walking past him and that gun. "My uncle might jazz talk to me but you're damn sure not", I rolled my eyes.

Heading to the car I saw my sister riding off with her new partner. It's crazy seeing a lot of people we grew up with still stuck in the game. Not too long after Dollah came walking out with his gun in his hand. "You better have all your pieces", I laughed getting in my car. He opened the door and got in. "Look before we pull off, put my shit back together", he said, dumping it onto my lap. It took me all of a few minutes to get it all back together. I smirked at him the whole time as he looked amazed. "Here crybaby", I said, tossing it back to him. "Yea whatever", he said. I pulled off, turning the music way up. Only for him to turn my shit down. "You know I could have put it back together myself but yo ass did it so", he said. "Umm excuse you I was listening to that", I turned to him. "How the hell are you supposed to know where we are going if you can't hear me", he threw his hands up. "Where to then", I asked smartly. "Look chill with the attitude girl", he responded. "Whatever", I rolled my eyes. "First, we have to go pick up this car from the airport. You will follow me to drop the car off at the destination. Then we will be making stops to get rid of what's going on in this trunk.

The car we are going to pick up has twenty keys in the trunk. So, make sure you stay on my ass till we get there", he instructed me.

I decided to take Kalamazoo to 44th street and take 44th all the way down. Leaving the music at a decent volume. Man, this dude was fine as hell. I kept trying not to look at his chocolate self. "So, Loyalty, how did you learn how to do what you did to my gun", he broke the silence. "Well growing up with the mother I had it wasn't my choice to learn", I said. "So how did meeting you get slipped up? "he continued. "I was off in college, maybe that's why, Envy didn't tell me about you either", I said. "Yes, cause I would have definitely remembered someone as beautiful as you", he grinned. "Well thank you", I smiled. "How did you get caught up into this family", I asked him. "When I was about thirteen, I had just gotten out of juvenile and your uncle took me in", he told me. "Oh really", I mumbled. "Yeah, and I've been around a little while that's why I'm shocked you were never mentioned to me", he looked at me. "Well, here I am in the flesh", I said smartly. "I definitely see you", he smiled. He was so handsome and smelled so good. "What is your major", he continued. "I was going to school for business management", I answered. "That's what's up so you wanna run a business", he asked another question? "You ask a lot of questions, you know that", I snapped. "Honestly Ma, I only asked a few and if I'm stuck working with you why not get to know you", he turned to me. "In that case yes, I do want to run a few businesses one day", I smiled at him. I pulled into the parking ramp once I got to the airport. He turned and smiled at me before telling me to park next to a black truck. "Aww shoot is that smile I see", he laughed. "Oh, hush where to next", I changed the subject. "We are headed to 52nd and Eastern behind the liquor store", he instructed. "Just follow close to me", he said. I headed in the direction behind him leading us to our next stop. Every stop he switched cars with a different driver. One thing I like is how he showed interest in what I was doing. That's very rare around here knowing the family business. He seems cool but I can't take any chances around here.

We hit about five more places before we headed back to see uncle QC. Pulling up to Envy standing on the porch talking on the phone. She seemed a little upset by the sound of her tone. "Before I go, meet me here tomorrow at nine am. We got a long day ahead of us, Dolla told me. I nodded in agreement. Getting out behind him as my sister walked up. He pushed her a little bit and she pushed him back. I could tell they were tight. "Stay out of trouble E call me if you need me", he said, getting in his car. Before he got in, we made eye contact and smiled at each other.

"So how was your first day back home," Envy broke my thoughts. "Boring as hell drove all damn day", I informed her. "Well get used to it sister you'll be driving awhile. Dollah jobs get a little dirty so you'll get some excitement", she told me. "What do you mean it gets a little dirty?", I asked? "He didn't explain to you what y'all doing. What the fuck was yall doing all this time", she rolled her eyes. "Is that your boo", I asked? "Girl no bitch that's my brother. Nothing going on period Loyalty", she laughed. I just looked at her shaking my head. Well at least he hasn't touched my sister because I'm definitely looking. "So, what do you mean then", I asked her? "Well sis Mr. Dolla is the realest I've ever ran across, he is most definitely about his money", she began to run down. "I can see that because we made multiple stops but he didn't let me go in", I told her. "Did it seem like he was making it look like he was alone", she asked? Now that I think about it, he did have a slick way of keeping me out of sight, thinking to myself. "Sis Dollah is our hidden weapon", she made eye contact with me. She sounded just like momma. Our mother kept her secret weapon close to her. The secret weapon was code name for assassin. So that meant he wasn't the one to fuck with. "He is dangerous and enjoys killing", she smirked. "Oh, really Momma would have loved him", I said. "Hell, yea like a queen on a throne stroking her vicious Pitbull", she responded. For some reason that turned me on. "Other than that, he is single and I hear he's slanging", she pushed me softly. I just smiled and told her "don't mix business with pleasure". "Yea whatever", she lit her blunt.

"So, you're staying with me at the house," she asked me? "I got reservations at the Amway for a month on unk, part of my agreement on being back here in this shit," I told her. "Well damn I'm staying the night with you tomorrow then," she insisted. "I'm going to hold you to it", I pointed to her. A white Benz soon pulls up in front of the house. "Who is this?", I asked? She turned around to look. "That's my ride duty called sister", she informed me and winked. "I'll call you in a minute big sis," she smiled. "Ok sis love you", I waved at her. She hops into the passenger side and they pull off music blasting.

Before going to the room, I stopped and grabbed something to eat. I grabbed a Tilapia meal from Four Brothers on Madison and Burton. It was slapping. I ran into a few people we knew from the neighborhood. I saw Gabe, Mook, Jerm, Tri and Bank posted in the parking lot. Then I walked into the store and saw Bud, Couch, Birthmark and Yum. I was shocked they remembered who I was. It's been so long since I've seen a lot of people.

Once I was in the room, I truly admired it. It was beautiful and the view of the city really captivated my attention. I made Uncle QC promise me a penthouse suit for a month, the majority of the money on a house, and a complete shopping spree. Oh yeah and all the money back that I paid for tuition. I wasn't taking a loss like that without gaining. My mother always told me "The person that makes you take an L, better take one too, or you damn sure better gain in the end." I really missed her so much she had an answer for everything. She was such a fierce woman and kept shit on lock.

After eating I watched the stars fill the sky as I sipped

on my wine. So much was going through my head. It really puzzled me to know who had enough heart to kill my mother. And why did QC really want me back here. I mean I know for damn sure he can control Envy. Well, it is my responsibility to watch over her. What is it that she was supposed to have done at the club he was talking about? I was so out of the loop but ready for whatever. When I finished the bottle, I went to run me a bubble bath. I was definitely about to enjoy this jacuzzi tub. Undressing and putting on the soft white rob they left for me. Soon as I was about to step foot into the tub a knock came at my door. Who the fuck could this be and what are they here for? I was so confused I hesitated to go to the door. Whoever it was knocked again. Tiptoeing towards the peephole to see. Lord behold it was Dollah. I flung the door open so fast. "If nothing is wrong with Envy you must have a damn good reason to be here", I scolded him. His ass just walks right in past me looking around. "Umm excuse me did you hear me", I said. "Girl hush all that shit up", he brushed me off. "Put this on time to go to work", he instructed me. "Niggah what", I folded my arms. "I said put the shit on in the bag, and let's go", he turned around. Staring at me with those sexy dark brown eyes that you could get lost in. This man was so fine it didn't make sense to me why he was a killer and not a model. "What do you mean, get dressed, do you know what time it is", I got pissed. "Look, Loyalty can just put the shit on and let's go damn", he pleaded. I snatched the bag from him and headed to the bedroom. "I'm about to use the bathroom, don't take too long ok", he yelled.

When I opened the bag it had a black hoodie, some black sweats with some all-black shoes. It also contained a black scully and black gloves. No need to ask what was going on now. I put everything from head to toe. I Pulled my hair into a ponytail and wrapped it into a bun. Walking out of the bedroom I was still puzzled about what we were about to do. He just stared at me for a minute quietly. As if he was truly admiring me, not even breaking eye contact. "Sorry I interrupted your bath. I'll make it up to you," he gestured. "Man, whatever let's go", I blew him off. "Let's go", he opened the door. "Leave your phone here," he told me. I set it on the table as we walked out.

We got into this all-black Mazda with dark tinted windows. The car reeked of weed I smelled getting in. "You and Envy with this damn weed", I shook my head. "Hell, you need to try some to relax your cocky ass", he giggled. He then handed me a 9mm handgun and a fully loaded clip. "I know you know how to use that right," he smirked. Holding it in my hand took me back. I remember one day I was putting it back together and decided to grab the trigger. I had to be about 11 years old. What I forgot was that it had a bullet in the head. So, I pulled the trigger and "Boom"! It had fired into the wall. My momma ran in there with two 357s pointing. I was so shaken up still holding the gun. After that she watched me shoot every weekend until I perfected it. "Of course, I do," I said, pushing the clip inside and cocking it back.

He pulls off turning his music up. I sat back and just rode along, the gun still in my lap. We pulled into this dark alley. This area was unfamiliar to me. Maybe because it was dark as hell not one light out here on. Parking in the abandoned garage, turning the car off. "Come on and stay close," he said, getting out. We crept down aways through the alley to a house close to the other end. "What the fuck is we doing", I whispered. "We're going to go in and lay everyone out. You watch my back as I grab the money. Before we run out, call me by the name "Blow and disguise your voice", he broke it down to me. "You showed me you can break a gun down, now show me how you bust that bitch", he laughed.

Creeping up to a black and white house with about 5 cars parked in the back. You can tell by the voices they were in the basement. It was a small window showing about six heads. Before kicking the basement door in he pulled another gun out. "So matching glocks huh", I whispered. "Just stay close and move quick", he whispered back. The next thing I knew we were downstairs with everyone at gunpoint. "Watch them stairs", he pointed with his gun. "Now somebody tells me where the money is or y'all all dying tonight", he yelled at them. These fools had to be in their early twenties. "We ain't giving you shit", one yelled back. "SMACK", he swung the gun. Busting the smart mouth fool in the head knocking him to the ground.

"I will kill everyone in this bitch quit playing with me", he told them. "Just tell him where the shit is Jay damn", one dude muffled. We were wasting time so I took over as if my mother was standing here. "Look all you muthafuckahs lay the fuck down now", I yelled. He looked over at me. "Yea get the fuck down bitches", he said again. They began getting down on the ground. "You over there come here", I said to the youngest looking one. He turned around and walked over. I took the gun and began beating him with it. The others instantly got nervous as hell. "Ok I'll tell you just stop hitting me", he pleaded. "Take me to the money now", I demanded. "If they move, shoot them", I told Dollah. He got up and led the way to the back room. I made him put everything into a gym bag laying on the floor. "Now let's go", I pushed him. We made it back out in front with everyone else and they were still laying there shaking. "You got it", Dollah asked? "Yea let's go", I nodded. "Wait", I stopped him. I turned around and put a bullet in everyone's head including the lil dog that I beat. We ran out the door down the dark alley.

Once we got back into the car he reversed and sped off. Making our way downtown to the parking lot of the Fish Ladder. He didn't say one word but kept looking over at me. My adrenaline was pumping so hard. I just killed four people and didn't feel any remorse. Maybe my mother passed the cold heart down to me as well. I was also scared as hell but didn't want him to see it. I avoided eye contact as much as I could.

We pulled up and parked the car. Not shortly after a white Benz pulled up. Envy hops out and greets us. "Is it done", she asked? "Yeah, all is well," he told her. She never acknowledged me at all but winked at me. "Come on", he motioned for me to follow. We got out and got into the Benz while Envy pulled off in the car, we were in.

Dollah took me straight back to the room. "Look I gotta come up and get those clothes from you," he said. I just nodded. We got onto the elevator in silence all the way up to the penthouse. I opened the room door and went into the room, shutting the door. I just couldn't hold it in anymore. Breaking down crying as I changed. What have I done? Who am I? So many questions filled my head. Not only did I kill for the first time, but I also killed four people. "Are you ok?", he said through the door. "No, I'm not ok", I sobbed in response.

Shortly after he came in and grabbed me by the hand. Leading me into the bathroom. He had re-ran my bath water with a wine glass next to it. "What's all this?", I asked? He had lit a few candles and all. "I told you I'd make it up to you", he smiled. His smile just eased my heart. "Well thank you but I just killed four people, not had a long day at work", I reminded him. "Loyalty this is your work now so relax ok", he said. I was so confused I swear. Did I just become uncle QC's secret weapon, I thought? He turned his back as I undressed and got into the water. "Here is some Remy, it will ease your mind", he handed me the glass. "I'll be out here when you get out. I'm going to crash here tonight", he informed me. Walking out shutting the door. I never had a man do this for me before. I was stirring away from love and lust by burying my head in my studies.

An hour passed and I had gotten out and wrapped my body in that cozy ass robe. Walking out to him sitting on the sofa watching tv, sipping a bottle. The table was covered with drugs and money. "You feel better. "he looked over at me. I didn't respond, I just stared. This very moment made me remember the first time I watched a man die. My mother had shot him dead. She didn't even care that I was in the room. Watching him bleed out his mouth and slowly stop breathing haunted my dreams for months. "Loyalty joined me", he patted the spot next to him.

I walked over slowly and plopped down. "Was this your first time Loyalty", he asked? "What do you think?", I said smartly. "Well, I don't know because Envy was busting guns young as hell", he answered. "Yes, this was my first time", I began to cry again. "Don't cry, fools have it coming "he handed me the bottle. I took the biggest gulp trying to make my mind as numb as my body. "Slow down", he said, grabbing it back. "I never wanted the lifestyle my mother paved for us. That's why I left and now I'm forced to be the killer I didn't know I was", I explained to him. Wrapping his arms around me, hugging me tight. "Loyalty sometimes the best thing for us to do is force out the real us", he whispered in my ear. I think this here Remy had me buzzing because I looked up at him and kissed him on the lips. He began kissing me back. We kissed about five minutes before I pushed him back. "I'm sorry I can't mix business with pleasure. Plus, my main focus is going back to school", I stood up. "Loyalty you yet seize to amaze me", he smiled. Puzzled at his admiration I walked off. Going into the room and shutting the door behind me. From the sound of me locking it gave him proof I wasn't coming back out or he was not coming in. He probably got multiple hoes and kids somewhere.

Laying there thinking about what happened and my mother till I finally fell asleep.

(Dollah)

I felt bad for dragging Loyalty into this. She truly shocked me tonight with her sexy ass. I couldn't believe how she handled herself. I also can tell how upset she was afterwards. Well, you can't run from what you were raised to be. She was different though; I mean I was really attracted to her. I want to get to know everything about her, I thought to myself.

Before going to sleep I hit Envy to make sure everything was good, and that we were headed in. Letting me know where she put the bags in the trap. See, Envy was like the little sister I never had. Even though her wild ass got on my nerves at times. I fucks with her heavily because she is a real solid chick. She doesn't play about the game either and will bust your ass quickly. One day Envy saved my life on the block. We were all shooting dice and me and some fool got into it. As I bent down to pick up my money, he put a gun to my head. He was all coked up and really fidgety. She walked into the alley at the right time. Two shots rang out and his body just dropped. That fool was about to blow my fucking head off.

I sat on the couch hoping Loyalty would come back out and talk to me. I decided to just fall back and leave her be for now. I can't believe she said she was single. Why hasn't anyone tried to wife her sexy ass up. Honestly, she doesn't deserve to be putting in work. She was supposed to be home reaping all the benefits from a good man. Tomorrow I'm going to talk to QC. He needs to send her back to school. She doesn't need this shit. Taking the last few shots before I went to sleep. First time all week I've been able to sit down. I live so far out I never be home. I had my house out in Standale. In a fully gated community of condominiums. I don't take no one with me to my crib. Well Envy has been there a few times but besides her no one must know where I stay at. Before I knew it, I felt myself dozing off.

When I woke up Loyalty was still sleeping. She must have gone to the bathroom in the middle of the night. Her ass finally unlocked the door. I peeked in before leaving. On my way out I wrote her a note. "When you wake up baby girl hit me asap, $" Placing it on the kitchen counter and heading out. I had to run home and clean up before getting to work in these streets.

(Loyalty)

I was awakened to the door shutting as if Dollah had left. Getting up to go and check. I noticed he was gone; I also noticed a note on the counter next to some money. I read the note and smiled, thinking about his kiss. Man, what am I doing here? I asked myself out loud, thinking about the boys I killed. I just don't get how my mother didn't have a conscience. She never showed emotion afterwards. Momma could kill someone and then take us for ice cream. It's like it gave her pleasure to end someone's life. "A waste of space", she always said afterwards. Momma was crazy in my eyes and I feared her more than the streets did. No matter who you were, you never disrespect momma period.

One day she had accidentally left her bedroom door cracked because she was cooking. Envy had to be about four or five, and she went in there. She poured a whole key of dope all over the room. Envy thought it was baby powder and began playing with it. Thank God, she didn't eat it or was harmed. Our mother walked in the room and went the fuck off. I wasn't even in there and got dragged into it. She beat our asses like really fucked us up. We stayed in our room where she left us for two days. Momma finally came back. She sat us both down and explained to us what she did. She also explained to us that Envy was playing with wasn't baby powder. "Look y'all I'm so sorry for putting my hands on you but stay the fuck out of that room. Only go in there if I tell you too, period", her words played back to me. Her mean ass didn't apologize for leaving us in the house though. After that very moment our relationship with her changed. Momma never hit us again and she kept us very close. She brought us so much shit to play with so the thought of fucking with her shit don't phase us. Then she began opening us up to drugs, sex, murder, and money. When I say sex, I mean momma even had a few hoes on the payroll. My momma had her hands in a little bit of everything.

I loved my momma so much. She was not the average momma but she can be labeled as the best to us. We never went without anything ever. Even when she did a lil bid that didn't stop her from making sure we were good. Going to the best schools, we both attended Grand Rapids Christian. Envy eventually got kicked out and went to Ottawa Hills. Don't let Envy fool you she smart as fuck and could of really went off to college with me. Envy's problem is that she wanted to be just like momma. Let me not mistake you. I definitely admire my mother just not for the same reasons my sister did. We definitely have the money fetish in common though. I must be mello like my daddy, it takes a lot to really upset me. But once I'm upset you could lose everything that means something to you and your life. After last night I knew I could kill again if I had to. It was something about the rush it gave me. Maybe it was the control and power I had over them, that turned me on. Then all of a sudden, I wasn't me anymore. Straight savage, my momma came out of me clearly. Sitting on the couch just thinking hard on my next move.

I decided I wasn't answering my phone or going outside today. Putting my phone on do not disturb and lying-in bed I gotta get my head right. I did just that too, I need today to be by myself.

3.

Don't Play With The Game

"Hey Envy come here", QC called out! "Yea", I walked into the room. "Where is Loyalty, I need to meet with yall", he asked? "She might be still in that room. You heard what happened, she was in shock", I told him. "Well, I gave her two days now, call her and Dollah, tell them to get their ass here", he said, lighting his cigarette. "Ok QC I got you", I rolled my eyes walking out. He always wants to talk to somebody, his ass starting to get on my nerves. Soon as I walked outside, I saw Dollah pulling up right on time. "Yo where is my sister at?", I asked walking up to him? "She must still be in the room. I haven't heard from her, he told me. "Well QC wants to meet with us all now", I said to him. "Did you call her", he asked? "I'm about to now", I grabbed my phone. It took her a minute to answer though but she finally did. "Wassup sis", she mumbled. "Where are you at sis", I asked? "I'm getting dressed", she informed me. "Well QC want you here asap at the spot", I told her. "Fuck QC I will be there in a minute", she snapped. "Ok sis just come on", I laughed. Her ass never really did like QC even as a child. She always told me he was a dirty ass dude. But her ass doesn't like anybody for real. I keep telling her ass to stop being so mean.

About thirty minutes later she pulled up. Giving me a hug as she walked into the house. My sister was something else you couldn't tell Loyalty nothing. Her ass was smart as hell and hid her dark side. I was gonna talk to her and see where her head was after we heard what this man wanted. "Come on sis let's see what's up", I waved at her. She followed behind me into the back room. When we get in, their QC is standing with his arms folded talking to Dollah. "Shut the door", he said. He then pulled out the duffle bag I put up last night. Pulling out about six keys and fifty thousand dollars. Sitting it on his little desk. "Good work last night", he smiled. "I hear you are quite the shooter", he looked at Loyalty. "What do you mean good work? Why am I really back here QC", she put her hands on her hips? "Last night was a test, the whole situation was a test", he told us. "I wanted to see how well you all would work together before I tell you my plans", he continued. Walking back and forth with his hands folded behind his back. QC must want a new territory or something. "What do you mean a test? Those boys last night lost their life over a test", she yelled. "Calm down Loyalty", he stood in front of her. "Them boys and many more are in our way of taking over the complete West side", he explained, rubbing his chin. "I know what you are capable of and it's time to help your family get ahead", he said to her. "Don't question me no more you hear me", he scolded her. "For the next few weeks shit gonna get real and I want y'all on tip", he told us. "What's our next job?", Dollah asked? I could tell Loyalty was pissed by the look in her eyes, she didn't need to say shit. "Give me a few days and I will get with you for the next job", he said. "I'm taking my lady friend out for a couple days so behave while I'm gone Envy", he insisted. I nodded but wasn't listening to his ass. "Hit me if need be y'all", he said, leaving.

"Let me treat y'all to something to eat", Dollah said to us. We ended up at Logans on 68th street. "Table for three please", I asked the waiter who greeted us. "Booth or table", she responded. "A booth is fine," I said. She walked us to the back booth against the wall. Loyalty sat next to me. Her and I both ordered some margarita drinks. Dollah lame ass just wanted a Sprite. We all ordered our food when she returned with our drinks. As we waited, I broke the silence. "So, Loyalty, I hear you are a natural-born gangsta sis", I laughed. "We're all crazy I guess", she sipped her drink. "Man, Envy what you think QC is up to", Dollah interrupted the conversation. "To be honest I'm thinking he is trying to take over the Cubans bro", I scratched my head. "The Cubans", Loyalty asked? "Yea that's one of the turfs momma used to want. To be honest, I think that's who took her out", I said. "I don't know but something just doesn't sit right with me though", Loyalty said. "Why all of a sudden go after it now all these years", she questioned? "I don't know sis but I do know one thing, they better be ready", I told her. "That part", Dollah agreed.

We received our food and it was so good. "Well duty calls", Dollah mentioned. "I'm going to take a lift from here," I told them. "Why", my sister asked? "I have to meet with a few people to get ready for the next hit and y'all gotta go across town," I answered her. "Well let's get moving Loyalty", Dollah stood up. "Call me if you need me", he said as they walked out. I sat and waited for my ride to arrive.

4.

A Long Time Coming

(Loyalty)

    As we rode around, I kept quiet for a minute just thinking. Then I finally broke the silence. "How long is this going to take?", I asked Dollah? "Why do you have somewhere to be?", he asked back. "Actually, I do. I would rather not spend my whole day riding in this damn car", I rolled my eyes. "What would you rather be doing, Loyalty am I boring you," he said. "Enjoying my day doing something else shit", I smartly said. "Look once I'm done making my rounds I'll take you to your car," he smiled. I sat back and folded my arms.

    "So, tell me Dollah what made you kiss me", I started a new conversation. "Honestly I don't know but I definitely enjoyed it", he told me. "I'm sure you got all the ladies chasing you", I fished for information. "Yea I'm a popular guy", he laughed. "Oh, you a male hoe huh", I looked at him. "I'm a single man with a lot of money and haven't run into the right woman", he smirked. "Yea ok", I replied. "I'm shocked to see you don't have a line of men chasing you," he said. "Whatever", I smiled. "No for real you're beautiful as hell and smart", he made eye contact with me.

"Unfortunately, the right one just hasn't presented himself to me yet", I told him. "Are you really a virgin Loyalty", he raised one eyebrow. "No, I just keep my shit on lock, I see too many girls ruin their lives for the wrong guy", I admitted. "How old are you?", another question came out of his mouth. "I'm twenty", I informed him. "How old are you?", I asked? "I'm twenty-three", he responded. "Yo that's very impressive that you're smart, beautiful and hood", he rubbed my shoulder. His touch was so soft and sincere. "Why thank you", I smiled.

He kept his word and took me to my car back at the trap. "I'll hit you later, you 're not off the hook that easily," he smiled. I got out and he pulled off. Just as I was walking to my car, I could feel someone's eyes watching me. I Looked around but didn't see anyone. Something just didn't feel right. I need to do some research on what's really going on around here. Since I was free the mall was my next stop. I decided to go shopping at the outlet mall Envy told me about. Putting the name into my GPS and heading that way. It only took about twenty minutes to get there. I'm glad it's nice out because I noticed that the store was outside.

I shopped for a little over an hour. It felt so good to get out and get my head right. Retail therapy is always best. Soon as I was walking to my car a guy stopped me. "Excuse me beautiful", he said. I stopped and turned around to acknowledge him. He was very handsome. Body covered in Nautica from head to toe. "Yes, can I help you", I responded. "What's your name sweetheart", he asked smiling. "Loyalty", I smiled. "So, you loyal huh", he smirked. "I'm Jordan" he introduced himself. "Well, what can I help you with Jordan", I asked. "I was wondering if I maybe had a chance to take you to dinner", he explained. He was cute and I really liked his smile so I agreed. "Sure, we can figure something out", I told him. He then grabbed my bags and walked me to my car. We exchanged numbers and I agreed to meet him tonight. Jordan asked me to dinner at Red Lobster at eight. I smiled and waved as I drove off.

Soon as my ass was getting on the highway heading home, my phone rang. It was Dollah. I made him wait a minute before I answered. "Hello"! "Wassup Loyalty, what are you doing"? "I just left the mall, why?", I told him. "I got a job for us tonight," he insisted. "Tonight, is not going to be good, can we do it tomorrow night," I said. "Why what you gotta do", he asked. "Well, I have a date tonight at eight and I don't wanna rush my time," I responded. "Well, you also have business to handle and I need you," he said. "Well Dollah, call Envy", I said and hung up.

Once back in the room I had to figure out what I wanted to wear. Since we were doing dinner and a movie, I figured it was sexy casual. Picking out three outfits and still couldn't choose. My phone began ringing and it was Dollah. Fuck that shit I'm about to enjoy my night. I didn't even bother answering, I told his ass my plans. I showered and sat on the bed in my towel still puzzled. One outfit was a Nautica dress, the second was a Tommy fit and the other was just some Rock jeans with a nice shirt. A knock came to the door. Walking over and looking through the peephole. It was my sister making goofy faces knowing I was looking. I opened the door and she walked in. "What are you here doing?", she asked? "Trying to figure out what to wear to my lil date tonight", I smiled. "Oh, so you got some action on the floor", she laughed. "Yes, I do", I rolled my eyes. "You serious aww shit check you out", she responded. "Can you help me out sis", I asked her? "Where y'all go", she asked? "To a movie and dinner", I explained. "It's easy sis wear the Nautica fit", she told me. "Yea I was thinking that too lil sis", I agreed. "So, who is the guy", she looks at me. "His name is Jordan. I met him leaving the outlet mall", I told her. "He better be fine", she laughed. "Girl don't do me", I responded. I began getting dressed and I decided to wear my hair down. "Can you flat iron my hair real quick", I asked her. "Yea I got you", she nodded while eating my food. "Go ahead, help yourself damn", I smirked. "Thanks, I'm high as hell", she kept eating.

I sat down for her to do my hair when Jordan texted me and canceled. I was so mad because I had gotten dressed for nothing. Envy phones kept ringing so she left right after she finished my hair.

Sitting on the couch looking all sexy for nothing. My phone began ringing and it was Dollah. "Hello", I answered! "Wassup Loyalty, where are you at", he asked?

"I'm in the washroom", I said. "I'm about to come grab you. We got a job in Muskegon," he told me. "Yea ok I'm ready", I informed him. Spraying my Gucci perfume and checking myself in the mirror. About ten minutes later he texted me to come on out.

When I walked out of the hotel, he was parked right at the front standing by the passenger door. As I approached the door, he grabbed the handle and opened it. Closing it behind me and heading back to get in. "Wassup", he greeted me! "Wassup", I responded. "How was your lil date", he spoke out. "I didn't go, he canceled last minute", I mumbled. "Oh, really he is a fool he lost", he smiled. "Why do you think it's his loss?", I asked. "Because you look fine as ever and smell so good", he looked over at me. I smiled at the thought of him admiring me. "Thank you", I smiled back at him. "I thought I was gonna have to come looking for you", he smirked. "Are we jealous?", I looked over at him. He didn't respond; he turned the music up instead. I could tell by his tone earlier over the phone he wasn't feeling it. I just sat back and rode along smiling at him every time I caught him looking.

(ENVY)

My ass is tired as hell. I need to lie down for a minute. I stopped at the trap and went to chill out. Smoking me a blunt and counting my money when I got in. Laying across the couch in the back room. Soon as I was dozing off, I heard someone come in. It was QC and someone else. I played sleep. I heard him tell them to go into his office. With me always switching whips he didn't even pay attention to the car in the front. His ass would have come and woke me up for something. They didn't close the door so I could hear them plain as day. Normally I leave when he has his meetings but today, I'm going to see exactly what is going on. It's too much fuckery and I'm so over QC yelling ass. If I could fix the problem maybe he would leave me be.

"So, QC what's up", the voice said. I couldn't put my finger on who that was just yet. I continued to listen. "We gotta get rid of his ass before he gets to the girls. He is back and stronger than ever, the voice said. "Look I got the girls on lock he can't get close to shit this way", QC responded. "You say that shit now but he is also coming for us too, he heard what you did", they said. "Look man, your job is to handle that and you better do so ASAP", QC told him. "If these girls find out anything then we're all dead you hear me so handle his ass and I'll handle them", QC spoke. "Lady never seen shit coming and neither will they", he laughed. Lady was my mother's street name, so I kept listening to the conversation. "Get back to work and hit me later I got a plan", QC told him. "Bet I got you big homie", the voice said. Just then I knew exactly who that was who he was conversing with. It was Spook ass; I wonder what was really going on. Me being me I climbed out the back window and ran to the front. I wanted to make sure who was really there. I sat on the front porch and lit my cigarette. My head was fuming boi I tell you. Just as

I expected they walked out. It was QC, Spook, and some other cats. Spook looked shocked to see me sitting here. The look in my eyes must have tipped him off. "Wassup fellas having a meeting without me", I smiled. "Wassup Envy", QC said, smirking. "Yo Spook got with me tonight I got something on the floor for us", I said to him. He nodded and held his head down walking to the car with the other dude. QC stood behind me for a minute. "Envy when did you get here", he asked? "I just got dropped off Unk", I lied. "Oh, ok come in let me holla at you", he said. "If I'm in trouble again, Unk can it wait I got a few moves to make", I told him. "Naw I just wanna holla at you so get ya ass in here", he walked in the crib. I finished my cigarette and headed behind him.

"Wassup Unk", I said, walking into the kitchen. "I want you to hang around here today and cook up a few bricks for me," he told me. "Then you and Loyalty are going to make the drop tonight picking up a few duffle bags ok." he looked at me. "Yea I got you just let me go handle this lil move and I'll be right back. Put everything in that spot and I'll have it done in no time, I informed him. "Ok bet I got new gloves and a mask under the sink", he pointed. "Ok bet." I nodded. He walked out and slammed the door.

I couldn't put my finger on what the fuk is going on but Loyalty and I better find out. Soon as I was walking out the door my homie Joe was pulling up. I walked over to the car and stopped him before he got out. "Bro took me to catch this jug and to the liquor store", I insisted. I got in the car and lit my blunt. "Wassup E you look stressed", he broke the silence. "Just got a lot on my mind today", I responded. I didn't want to mention anything to no one until I talked to my sister. "How long were you at the spot", he asked? "I had just landed," I told him. "What were you on?", I asked him. "Just was trying to catch up with QC", he told me. "Aww yea you had just missed him", I said. "Damn he is a hard man to get a hold of", he shook his head. "Hell, yea he is", I agreed. I caught my play at the store so I had him drop me back off.

Rolled me a few Ls, poured me a drink, and headed to the kitchen. My mind was still puzzled and I wanted to know what QC was hiding. I needed to get back on his good side. Turning on that Mozzy and getting straight to it. Before turning on the stove, I made sure all the doors were locked. Those who need to get in have a key.

(Loyalty)

We hopped off the highway and headed to the house Dollah said we had to hit. "Umm I'm not dressed for no hit right now", I told him. "Yea I know but you good I just need you to watch my back and drive. "I want you to knock on the door and keep this fool distracted until I slip in through the back", he informed me. "Once you in then what", I asked? "I'm going to slit his fukin throat that's what", he explained. "Who is he", I continued? "Some cat that QC got smoke over some turf. I have been watching him for months so please be on point", he told me. "I got you dang ain't nobody going to mess shit up", I smirked.

Grabbing the gun, he handed me and put it into my purse. Applied some more lip gloss and popped some gum into my mouth. "Now watch me work", I giggled. Getting out and walking towards the door. As I knocked, I saw him run to the back yard. Sexy ass I thought to myself. Not soon after a Cuban guy came to the door. "Can I help you lady", he asked? Looking me from head to toe. "Yes, I'm new to the area and gotten lost", I thought of something quick. From where I was standing, I could see Dollah sliding through the patio door. "Where are you trying to go mam", he asked me? "Back towards the highway", I said. Well, yes you are lost I'm about fifteen minutes from the highway, " he told me. "Do you mind if I use a phone and use the bathroom", I asked him? "Sure, come in beautiful and make it quick ok", he instructed me. Following him inside and to the bathroom. I noticed blood on the sink in the bathroom. It looked as if it was fresh too. I played it off and came out. Heading back down the hallway towards the front room. Before I knew it someone had grabbed me and threw me in the back room. It was the man who let me in. "What are you doing?", I asked, trying to get loose. "I saw the way you looked at me when I opened the door," he smiled. "What the fuk is you talking about", I yelled. "Let me go now", I screamed. He then slapped the shit out of me and I fell to the bed. He climbed on top of me and began trying to get my pants off. He had ripped my shirt completely. "STOP please STOP", I cried. I was so scared this had never happened to me before. He was so strong too; my purse fell off the bed. I was trying to reach it but he had begun choking me. Feeling myself lose consciousness, I couldn't breathe. "Stop fighting and take this gift I got for you. This man was really trying to rape me and where the hell is Dollah. I let out one more big scream and boom the door flung open. "BAM, BAM, BAM", Dollah shot the gun. Shooting him three times. Running over to me and picking me up and throwing me over his shoulder. I was still trying to catch my breath. Once we were outside, he gave me the shirt off his back. "You ok Loyalty", he asked. Fighting back tears I nodded in agreement. "Come on", he waved. We ran to the yard over and walked around that house so no one would see us coming from his house. Hopping in and pulling off fast. "Where were you? " I yelled at him. He pulled over around the block, and I began to hit him repeatedly. He grabbed me by the arms to get me to stop swinging. "Calm down Loyalty please", he pleaded. I finally took a deep breath and stopped hitting him. I was so mad I could kill the world. "Something ain't right", he said, pulling off. "What you mean", I asked him. In the meantime, I was texting my sister to tell her what the fuck just happened. "I mean it's like he knew we were coming," he slapped the steering wheel. "Who the fuck could have tipped him off?" I responded? "I don't know but damn sure about to find out," he said. Before I can say another word, he turned the music up. I can't believe that muthafuckah tried to rape me. The way his ass burst through the door turned me on. I mean his sexy chocolate self was looking like superman. I turned his music down to let him know where Envy wanted him to bring me. He didn't say a word, he just nodded, turning the music back up.

We made it back in town quickly. I can see the smoke coming from his ears, I swear. We pulled up to a house off of 60th and Division. Envy was standing on the porch smoking a cigarette. I got out and he didn't even say a word. He put the car in reverse and pulled out the driveway. Blowing the horn twice at Envy. She threw her hands up in response to him.

5.

Time to turn it up a Notch

I walked up to the porch and she rushed me. Checking me from head to toe and hugging me. "I'm ok Envy", I assured her. When I say she acted just like my mother she doesn't want to hear nothing. "Who the fuck and what the fuck happened", she yelled. "I don't know sis for real", I said. "All I know is we went to a hit. We set our movements up to a T so I thought. I played the front while Dollah snuck in the back", I explained. "So how did he end up putting his hands on you", she asked? "Once I got in, I played it off saying I had to go to the bathroom, so Dollah could look around. Well, he had me fooled because when I walked out of the bathroom, he grabbed me. Pushing me into the room and tried to rape me". "So, where the fuck was Dollah at", she asked. "He busted in and that was the end of that sis". She just stood there with the look of a true killer. "But something strange is going on. I know that", I told her. "Why do you say that sis?", she turned to me. "Dollah said it seemed like he knew we were coming", I informed her. "No wonder why he spread off like that," she replied. "Yea he was pissed off Envy". "If someone was tipped on to him being a hitman that jeopardizes everything", she continued. "Remember what momma said about your secret weapon being exposed", she reminded me. Thinking back to when my mother had a talk with us. We were in the car and she dropped some money off to a short dark-skinned man. As I can remember she would always only make drop offs for him with money. "When your secret weapon is exposed, it could jeopardize everything. Your secret weapon was a very valuable piece of the puzzle", she told us. Our mother didn't hesitate to tell or let us see anything. That was her worst decision as a mother if you ask me. "Loyalty quit daydreaming. Are you listening to me", she snapped at me. "Yes, I'm listening. Question is are you paying attention to shit going around you?", I snapped back at her. "QC said I had to come home to get you back on track", I told her. "You fell for that dumb ass shit", she laughed. "Yea he told me that you were getting out of hand and all that momma had built was at risk". "Loyalty now you know better than that, come on now", she smirked. "Envy momma put her blood, sweat and time into building all this", I reassured her. "You think I don't fucking know that like for real. I'm the one who set my life aside to keep this shit rolling. You shot out the first chance you got", she walked into the other room. "Envy, what are you mad at me for? I didn't ask to be your babysitter", I followed behind her. "Loyalty fuck you for real. I don't need no fuckin babysitter", she waved me off. This girl about to piss me the fuck off. "Envy on some real shit you're grown as hell now. Just like I am, I don't need to watch you. But you are my little sister and I am responsible". "What you fail to realize is this shit deeper than you think", she replied. "What do you mean tell me what the fuck going on then. I mean what the fuck we are sisters and momma raised us better than this arguing shit", I yelled. She sat down at the kitchen table and began rolling up. "Momma wouldn't be pleased with us arguing", she smirked. "Hell, naw we would be getting cussed the fuck out", I sat down across from her.

Our mother didn't play that bickering shit. She had zero tolerance for sibling rivalry. Sometimes she lets us talk shit to each other but it better be brief. She taught us that people say the most hurtful shit when they are mad. Always reminding us that she grew up alone until we came. Making sure that we knew how short life was and we only had each other. Right before she died her conversation with us was so deep. We were all sitting at home on the couch. Momma was sitting in the middle of us both. She had decided to stay in and kick it with us. "I want you to know that I love you both very much. Yall are the two most important people in the world to me. I know I'm not the best mother in the world, but I damn sure made sure y'all had love. Growing up for me was not easy. I was tested way too young and ended up acing the SAT (Street Affiliated Teaching). I want y'all to have more out of life than I did. Also, no matter what you do in life, focus. Even if you follow in my footsteps, be nothing less than me. I named y'all Loyalty and Envy for a reason and its meaning to that. Loyalty, I gave you that name because that holds everything together with no glue. Envy I named you that because when it comes with power and will wreck shit with vengeance", she explained to us. Our mother's real name was Promise aka Lady P. She hated her name but never told us why. "No matter what life throws at y'all hold it down together. Even when I'm dead and gone, never let no one come between y'all", she told us. As she was talking to us tears flowed down her face. "I truly apologize for the stuff y'all have had to witness. Momma has to do what she has to do", she sobbed. Hugging us so tight and kissing our foreheads. That was the last real conversation we had with her. She was killed my senior year in high school. I was seventeen years old. All I remember is that she was moving real fast that day in and out. Envy was at basketball practice. I was home cleaning my room. She walked in and sat some money on my dresser. "Loyalty grab y'all a pizza tonight ok", she told me. "Alright momma, where are you going? "I asked her. Usually, she would get mad at us asking her do's and whereabouts. "I gotta go make this run for QC cause he's out of town", she informed me. "Aww ok", I started sweeping. "I'll by the time I think Envy made it home", she walked out. She came back into the room and spoke to me. "Loyalty, I love you and you are responsible for you and your sister," she smiled so pretty. "I love you too momma and I know", I smiled back. When I heard the door slam behind her when she left the house. I never knew she wouldn't walk back through it again.

Envy made it home just as I was ordering the pizza. "Hey, you know where momma is at sis", she asked? "Naw not since earlier why", I said. "Well, I've been calling her for the last hour and she didn't answer or call back yet", she plopped down on the couch. We sat and sat waiting on her. I knew something wasn't right because she wasn't answering her phone. No matter what momma always answered for us or called right back instantly. The next morning QC came in and delivered the bad news. My world had then been snatched from me and I couldn't understand why. I know momma did a lot of dirt but damn why did y'all have to shatter our world along with hers. Envy hearts had turned so cold as if they became Antarctica itself. I truly hurt more for her because she is what slowed momma down a lot. We all were close but they were close. That's why we always said she was the splitting image of her. Envy lit her blunt and just sat here. "Envy listen I got your back right or wrong. We have each other no matter what", I assured her. "I know sis you're about the only one I trust", she responded. "Loyalty, listen to me sis I think you have been right all this time", she told me. "About what sis", I was confused. "I think QC on some bullshit. Shit just not sitting right with me". "What do you mean"? "Well, I overheard him having a conversation with some dude and Spooks. They were talking about us. Someone is trying to get close to us and he is trying to stop them from informing us of some shit. It seems like QC wants to get rid of us both", she explained to me. I never liked his old ass. QC always gave me a snake-like vibe. He got another thing coming if he thinks it's going to be that easy to take shit. "Look Envy we need to get rid of his ass and anybody else that rolls with his ass. Take back what our mother built", I said. "You want to go against QC", she looked up at me. "Hell, yea and we're gonna do it but very discreetly. We're gonna come up with the best plan. He won't know what hit him", I rubbed my hands together. "I'm rockin 'with you but we definitely need a solid plan. Only a few people will go up against him," she told me. "Give me some time to put some shit into play and I will tell you exactly what we will be doing". I explained to her. "So just continue to play the same role until then ok Envy", I looked at her. "Yea I got you", she agreed. "I'm serious Envy, I know you're mad but stay calm for a minute".

Her phone then started ringing. She smiled when answering it so I knew what that meant. "Hey sis, make yourself comfortable this is my crib," she told me. 'Where are you going? " "Nowhere just about to have some company for a little while," she smirked. "I got firestick, Netflix, and whatever else you might wanna watch in the living room," she informed me. "So, this is your place sis", I finally repeated. "Hell, yea bought and paid for," she smiled. Grabbing her rellos and weed she headed out of the kitchen.

I couldn't help but to think about everything going on. What the hell did I come home to? Dollah being upset was on my mind as well. I decided to call and check on him. His phone went to voicemail, I called twice. I was puzzled why he was reacting like he was. Shit I was the one who was damn near rapped. Headed into the living room to sit on the couch. I could hear sis and her friend talking. Me being nosey I listened for a minute. They were talking about stuff that I would have never thought my sis was interested in. Had me cracking up gone sis do your thang. Turning the tv on looking for something to watch. Ended up picking a movie called True To The Game. A girl from school told me to watch it before I left. I was really missing school; I wasn't too far from graduating. QC got me messed up and it's time I turn it up a notch.

6.

Tell Me Something Man

(Dolla)

What the fuck really going on man. I wrecked my brain sitting in my car. It really seemed as if this fool knew we were coming. I felt so bad that he even got the move on Loyalty. The question is who could have tipped him off. The only people that knew about petty hits were Envy, Spook and QC. Now my major hits like this only QC or Envy knows. I don't think they would play me like that. If somebody tipped my hits, they could blow my whole shit. Nobody knows that I'm the one they call Casper the boogieman. I developed that name by coming for your ass like a thief in the night. You could look at me and tell me that I was your worst nightmare. I gotta change everything. Get rid of this phone, switch up whips and make a new routine. In the meantime, find out what the fuck going on. Play my part and get some answers because if what I think is going on we have a problem. Call QC because we need to talk ASAP. He told me to meet him at the diner Shelly's on Burton and Michael street. I headed on route as soon as we hung up.

It only took me about fifteen minutes to get there.

Making sure my gun was loaded and off safety. Right now, I gotta watch everyone and everything. I Walked in and noticed him sitting in the back booth. I joined him at the table being very observant. "So, what did you need to talk about that couldn't wait until I ate", he sipped his coffee. "Some shit went down yesterday that didn't sit right with me", I jumped right to it. "What happened? I heard the hit was a success", he rubbed his hands together. "Man, it seemed as if he knew I was coming. He tried to rape Loyalty", I explained. Watching his reaction. "What you mean rape Loyalty", he sat back. "Yea we had shit planned for a T but the whole time he was onto us. Now after all the years I've worked for you I know somebody didn't tip my hit. That would mean someone either is on to me or someone wants me dead", I stared at him. "So, what are you saying Dolla?", he asked me. "I'm saying what the hell is going on", I sat back as well. "Look honestly I think Envy is trying to take us down," he told me. "What", I asked? "Yea she's been off the chain lately. I think she wants to shut her own mother's business down. I'm looking into this and I will find out who was behind that bullshit", he informed me. I was in shock when he said Envy may be the one who tipped the hit. Something is really going on and I can't get caught up into it. "So, you think Envy is trying to take us out", I repeated what he said. "Yeah, I got some people looking into it", he sipped his coffee again. "Look cool out for a minute until I figure this out. Also keep your ears and eyes to the street, ' he told me. His demeanor seemed a little off but I agreed. "Now let me get back to my meal", he smirked. "Alright I'll see you later to give you my new number", I said. He nodded and went back to eating. I headed to my car sitting for a minute while I rolled a few blunts.

I can't picture Envy being behind this. Don't get me wrong I know she is wild but she is not that wild. She has never shown me no disloyalty ever. Something telling me QC on some bullshit I've been around him for too long to not notice. Then on the other hand she has been flipping out a lil bit more than usual. I can't say who was in the wrong at the club because I got there right after. She did tell me that QC sent her there to meet someone, and she ended up getting into a shootout. I need to holla at her ass to see where her head is at. Me and Envy are too tight for her to risk it all like this. Also, if it is QC, she needs to know I got her back against his snake ass. This man is trippin 'if he was one like that. I remember stories about him he doesn't know. Like he may be the one who had something to do with their mother getting killed.

When I was little my mother and her friend were sitting on the porch talking. I was sitting on the couch playing the game while listening. Our window did not have a screen so you could be very clear. My mom friend said her and QC was fucking around and he was always putting his sister down. She said sometimes it got so bad he would be so upset he would fuss all the time. He hated how close she was getting with the Cubans after the beef they carried. He hated that she went as far as having two kids by one. I didn't know who QC was personally but I definitely knew who Envy momma was. I wanted to get money with her so badly. Not long after she had gotten killed QC approached me about working for him. I was about twelve years old. He raised me up in a different town after my mom died from an overdose. I was actually young as hell with my own crib plushed out. Teaching me how to be a killer, basically how to be the best hit man I could be. One thing he knew was that he created a monster and I didn't hold him up either. He had a way of bullying a muthafuckah to do what he says. Whoever is behind this got a serious issue on their hands from me though.

Once I had my blunts rolled up, I headed to the phone store. Then I'll go get dressed, grab Loyalty, and do our rounds. I hope she has calmed down by now. She was really shaken up but I don't blame her. I gotta also see where her head is at as well. She has to be ready at all times when we are too deep to be slipping and shit. I need her on point at all times. I also need to watch her ass just in case Envy is on one because she is rolling with her sister. Man, this crazy and I'm not going out that easy.

I need to get some info on QC though and know just who to talk to. My grandfather knows him very well. He just doesn't know that it is my grandfather. I will definitely go talk to him. My grandfather is a retired hustler named Dice. He used to hang around QC growing up. I know he can shed some light on what I am up against. Matter of fact, I'll go by tomorrow. Let me get these drop offs ready and grab Loyalty. I'll text her after I get my new phone.

(Loyalty)

I dozed off quickly. I noticed when my phone rang. It was a number I didn't know but I answered anyway. "Hello", I answered! "Yo this Dollah I'm about to slide on you", he told me. "Ok cool I'm still where you left me but I need to go get dressed", I told him. "Ok bet I'll be there in twenty minutes," he said. We hung up and I went upstairs to let my sister know I was leaving. I knocked on the door a couple times before she opened it. "Wassup sis", she poked her head out. "I'm about to go get dressed and ride with Dollah," I told her. "Alright just get up with me tomorrow", she smiled. "Ahh shit so you locked in for the rest of the day," I smirked. "Yea and tomorrow I'll have a key for you to come here, fuck that hotel shit ya hear me". She sounded so much like my momma. "Ok lil sis I love you", I kissed her forehead through the door. "Love you too," she replied.

Walking back downstairs to turn everything off before he pulled up. Not shortly after he was pulling into the driveway. I yelled upstairs for Envy to come lock her door. She yelled back at me to twist the bottom lock. When I got into the car Dollah was looking as sexy as usual. Opening the door asking him before getting in, "You ok now". "Yeah, I'm good, get in we gotta go", he waved at me. Getting in and buckling up as he pulled off. I was shocked he didn't turn the music up like always.

On our way to the room, he eventually broke the silence. "Loyalty are you ok", he asked? "I'm ok. I was shaken up but I'm good," I responded. "I called you to check on you but I got no answer," I told him. "Well, I got rid of those phones. So, store that number in ok", he said. "I want to apologize for not getting in there right away, I wouldn't have been able to forgive myself if something happened to you," he told me. We pulled up the room. "You come up while I get dressed," I asked. "Yea come on don't take long," he smirked. "Whatever", I laughed.

We made it up to the room and he waited on the couch as I showered. While I was in the shower, I thought about what me and Envy talked about. I knew I had to step my game up and get my hands dirty. Starting with getting Dollah on my side because if he was working with QC he was just as dead to me as his ass was about to be. It was time to turn shit up and get my hands all in the mix. Put forth what my mother installed into me. Plus, I wanted this man so bad and was ready to see just exactly what was attracting me. The angle of the bathroom gave me a clear view of him from the living room. I admired him from a crack in the door. He was sitting there looking like a whole snack. Chocolate himself looked so delicious in his red and black. That read beater hugged his body so well. Six packs busting through it as well as their chiseled arms. The bulge in his black basketball shorts showed he was blessed below. I was nervous but ready to see what the hype was about. I sprayed on my perfume and slipped my robe on. "Girl, will you hurry up? We have so much to do," he yelled. I bet we do, I said, looking at myself in the mirror. I was horny as hell and wanted him since the day I laid eyes on him. I knew he wanted me back. I pulled my hair into a ponytail.

Opening the door to the bathroom and taking a deep breath before I did what I was thinking. Walking over to him slowly, watching him the whole way. He kept his eyes glued to me as I headed his way. "What is taking you so long?", he asked? "You can't rush perfection", I smiled. Straddling him as I leaned in to kiss him. He wraps his arms around my waist and kisses me back. Slowly moving his hands up and down my body. His touch felt so good, hands so soft and gentle. I rocked back and forth against him as we kissed. I then soon felt his manhood stand at attention. "You ready for this," he whispered in my ear. "Are you ready for me?", I responded. "Oh, girl I've been ready", he stood up. Holding me in his arms. Wrapping my legs around his waist as he carried me towards the room. Laying me on the bed as he untied my robe. I could feel myself getting turned on more and more. My pussy was super wet. He rubbed his fingers through it and then sucked them. That drove me wild. "It tastes good doesn't it". He sat there for a minute and admired my naked body under this robe. I sipped it off and threw it to the floor. He then lifted his shirt above his head and allowed his shorts to hit the ground. His dick was standing at full attention behind those Polo draws. He was definitely working with a monster. I can't wait to feel him inside me. Leaning in on top of me. Kissing my neck so softly as he caressed my body. Closing my eyes, enjoying every bit of it, as he sucked on my nipples. Letting out a soft moan as he kissed my stomach. It tickled a little. Grabbing my legs, spreading them far apart. Leaning in, licking my inner thighs. Sending chills up my back. Feeling his tongue sliding across the lips of my vagina made me clothes my eyes and take a deep breath. Gripping his head as he made love to my pussy using his lips and tongue. Caving my back in as he sucked on my clit. Oh my God he knew exactly what he was doing. My legs began to shake but that didn't stop him. I moaned out loud as I felt my body coming. Moving his tongue faster caused me to cum so hard. Finally lifting his head up beard covered in my juices. He stood up and dropped his draws. Revealing that third leg of his standing strong. Grabbing the rob to wipe his face. Placing a condom over his dick as he moved in on top of me. Slowly putting himself inside. Taking a deep breath as I expected him inside. Slowly grinding my hips against him. Grabbing one of my legs and placing it across his shoulder. Watching himself go in and out makes me unable to hold my composure. I began to moan louder as he pushed deeper while biting his bottom lip. His reaction was showing me that he was really enjoying me. Rubbing his finger across my clit as he moves faster in and out. He caused me to squirt and climax back-to-back. "Oh, shit yessss", I moaned. "Turn over", he instructed me. I did as I was told, putting that arch in my back to work. He grabbed a pillow and placed it under my waist. Slowly sliding into me from the back. I gasped as I took him all in. He had my juices flowing so well. I don't know what he was doing to me but I was really enjoying it. Moving in and out gripping my ass as he pushes deeper each time, he stokes in. Having me biting the sheets and climaxing back-to-back. Leaning more on my back moving in and out faster and faster. Digging his nails into my cheeks. He let out a deep breath. I looked back at him and encouraged him. "Yes, baby fuck me", I moaned. He pounded a few more times and then exploded. Smacking my ass before collapsing next to me. "Damn girl this pussy is good as hell", he said catching his breath. I began kissing his chest making my way down to his limp dick. Grabbing it and putting it into my mouth. It didn't take long before it was back on hard. Moving my head up and down caressing him tight with my lips. Twisting and turning my tongue on his tip. He slid my ponytail holder off rubbing his hands in my hair. Sucking and slurping him like he was my favorite popsicle. He was letting out soft moans. "Damn that's how you're going to do me", he gasped. I just kept slobbering all over him. I felt his leg starting to shake so I took one of my hands and stroked him. Still sucking up and down, staying focused on the tip of his dick. Before I knew he burst in my mouth I swallowed and kept sucking. He was going crazy trying to push me away. I kept going long enough to get him hard again. It was time for the home run. I climbed on top of him and took off. Riding him as if he was my own personal horse. Holding his chest and biting my lip. Rocking back and forth keeping a circular motion. So caught up in the moment I didn't give him time to put on another condom. This dick was feeling so good it was too late to turn back. Bouncing faster and faster as he held my waist lifting me up and down. Pushing himself up to go deeper. I felt myself about to cum. My legs were getting weaker and weaker the more I moved. This was one of the best orgasms I ever had. When I say we must have been on the same page. He flipped over on top of me and held one of my legs in each of his hands. Pushing inside me deeper and deeper faster and faster. Cause me to not hold my screams any longer. "Yesss baby yessss", I moaned. "Ummm oh shit", he moaned back. We came so hard together I felt his juices fill my walls. I just closed my eyes and came so hard that I squirted. He collapsed on top of me still keeping his dick inside. Both trying to catch our breath, my legs were shaking so bad. "I have never been fucked like this", I whispered in his ear. He looks up at me and said, "I will fuck you better every time". Kissing me so passionately and sincerely. I was not expecting this but I loved every moment of it.

We both got in the shower together dressed and got to work. While we were in the car, the ride was silent for a minute. We just kept looking over at each other smiling. Dollah didn't know it but he was mine from that moment forward.

(Dollah)

I don't know what the fuck just happened but it was amazing. Loyalty just rocked my world just as I thought. I mean it was way better than I thought it would be. She was not going anywhere, that lil pussy got some power. I still wasn't supposed to go in raw and bust in her. I shook my head to myself. I looked over at her and couldn't stop smiling. Her head game was the best I had thus far and I've had plenty of it you know. It was so hard to not think about wanting to fuck again. Dick getting hard just thinking of being inside her. It was really hard trying to not focus on her fine ass sitting next to me. Soon as these drops are done, I'm on her ass. "So, Dollah, what did you mean by someone may have tipped him off", she asked me? "When I said that I meant just what it sounded like Loyalty". `Somebody had to tell him we were coming. I say that because it was just too easy to get in. I have watched this man and he is never home alone. He has dogs too; they never came out. Plus, the patio door was cracked", I explained to her. "When I made it to the room to look around, that's when I heard you" I said. "Yea he moved in on me quick", she said. "Look I think QC is up to no good", she turned to me. "What do you mean"? "I don't know just yet but I think his ass is trying to eliminate my sister and I," she continued. "Word is some Cubans are trying to get in contact with us and he is blocking hard", she went on. "You really think that he would do that", I asked her? "Hell, yea I never trusted his ass `from a child", Loyalty continued. "All I know is that the only people who knew about that hit was QC, Envy, and Spook", I informed her. "Well, whatever the fuck going on I will find out", she told me. "Yea we most definitely are going to find the fuck out", I agreed.

A few people I know can probably get us a meeting. Just gotta let this shit cool down I thought to myself. She may be onto something about QC. I'm for sure going to check into this shit ASAP. We headed to do a few more drops when I got a call back from my grandfather. He told me to come by and talk to him. He must have got that message I sent his way. "You hungry Loyalty", I asked her? "Yea kinda
, she replied. "Ok but after this last drop. We can grab something," I told her.

After we ate, I took her with me to talk to my grandfather. He stayed out in Standle with me as well. Not in the same house but the same town. I had him meet up at my spot, without letting her know this was my crib just yet. I didn't even tell her he was my grandfather. I trust her and all but until I know what's going on I need some insurance. I say that because my grandfather never forgets a face. Maybe that's where I get it from. So, if it is Envy plotting on me then she just signed her sister's death certificate.

We ended up pulling up at the same time. "This is my old head, he cool people", I informed her. "Aww ok he got a nice ass Lac", she sat up. "Yea he got a few of those",

I smirked. "Come on," I motioned to her. Getting out of the car we headed into the house, following behind my grandfather. He went straight into the office area. Allowing Loyalty to walk in first and I followed behind her. "Hey, their young blood", he greeted me! "Wassup with it pimpin", I said back. We both smiled at each other. "Who's your lady friend", he asked me? Looking Loyalty up and down with admiration in his eyes. I clear my throat to get his attention to back off that way. "I'm Loyalty and you are", she spoke up. "You can call me old school", he introduced himself. "Who might be comfortable with talking in front of her"? "Would you believe me when I say this is my new partner and oldest daughter of Lady", I stared at him. "Oh my God this is don't tell me", he rubbed his head. "This is Loyalty", he smiled. "Yes, that's me," she smiled. "I haven't seen you since that day your mother cut out Smooth B tongue. I ended up going to prison for a while after that", he explained to us. "Yes, then that definitely was a long time," she responded. "Your mother and father were about to take over the whole damn city until QC snake ass got in the way", he went on talking. The look on Loyalty's face showed the confirmation she needed to hear.

"So, Ol' Skool you say QC a snake", I sat down. Showing that she had her full attention on him she sat next to me focused. "You knew my mother", she asked him? "Yea I knew her since she was a child running recklessly in these streets", he told her. "I met her maybe a week after being on the run from the foster home she was in. It was raining hard outside and she was posted up on Burton and Eastern. I was sitting in my car across the street in the Health Food Store parking lot, watching the strip. A car pulls up and some niggahs pull up trying to rob her. She whipped out her tool and busted their asses. I knew then she wasn't going to hold these streets up", he told us. "What did you do?", she asked him? "What you mean is what he does Loyalty", I butted in. "My mother always told me if she left someone around to tell a story about her, they gotta be solid", she explained.

"Your mother was the finest thang walking. Then she had so much power at a young age which made her even more sexy. We did a lot of business together, " he told us. We sat back and let him tell his story. I'll ask some questions in a minute. Loyalty and Envy had this same very discreet look when they were silently angry. "So why do think you QC a snake", she asked him? "QC talks a good game but he gets high off his own low key and only cares about himself," he filled us in. "All those years of getting high catching up to him," he told us. I never knew he was getting high; he damn sure hides it well. We continued to listen to him break it down. "QC was a beast growing up, everyone feared him and your mother. You couldn't pay a soul to breathe hard against them two, he continued. "Well QC decided to try his own product and was caught by your father. He mentioned it to your mother and she flipped out. I guess she had noticed shit was getting shorted but didn't know from where, " he told us. "I kinda remember her and him having a big fight and we didn't see him for a while," she interrupted. "They had many fights but this particular fight happened right before she passed", he looked up at her. "So, you're telling me he had something to do with my mother's death", she asked? "From my point of view if he didn't pull the trigger himself then he had it done Loyalty", he stood up. She sat there with a look of defeat plastered all over her face. I hate that she had to hear this but my grandfather wasn't called to know it all for nothing. "Your mother found out the truth about what QC had done to your father and shit hit the fan", he told her. "What did he do", she asked? "Well, your father was the one who taught your mother everything she knows. QC hated him for whatever reason. I'm thinking over your mother. Everyone knew QC wanted to be with her but she was not feeling that shit", he smirked. "I think they messed around a few times though but not too sure", he lit his blunt. "After your sister came shit hit the fan. Rumor was that Envy should have been his child". "What", she gasped. "Yea and to be honest I think he started that rumor. But who really knows", he shrugged his shoulders? "Why did my dad leave"? "QC ass told your mom that he was cheating and had a family in Cuba. Your momma wasn't having that shit. So, she ended up shooting at his ass", he laughed. "I don't mean to laugh but your mother was crazy as hell," he chuckled. "Yea she definitely was," she smirked. "Look we're gonna have to finish this conversation another time", he said. "Why what's up Ol Skool", I asked? "I have an important meeting in a minute and nobody needs to be here," he informed us. "Will you be willing to talk to my sister and I together please", she asked? "Well, I guess I can talk to yall but it has to be another time. Come by Friday afternoon and bring a small fee, he smirked. He then walked us to the door.

The car ride was silent as hell. I really didn't know what to say. "You ok Loyalty", I broke the silence. "Yea I'm good but just know all hell is about to break loose. You either with us or get rolled the fuck on too", he replied. "What do you mean get rolled on", I snapped. "You heard what the fuck I said Dollah if you apart of this shit I will blow your ass myself", she repeated. It was as if she was another person. "I'm gone tell you like this don't you ever fucking threaten me again", I yelled. "Fuck you and all that yelling you heard me muthafuckah", snapped back. "Dumb bitches took my momma from us, I'm taking the whole city out", she mumbled. Loyalty was on a whole different level but I'm definitely riding with them. I just don't take kindly to threats. "I don't know what you are planning but you better have a rock-solid plan. Don't let your emotions get the best of you, "I told her. She didn't respond; she kept looking out the window. I was worried that she would handle this the wrong way and get herself killed. After doing a few more pickups I dropped her off to the room. Before getting out she told me to meet her over at her sister's house in two hours. I agreed.

7.

You Done Fucked Up

(Loyalty)

I paced back and forth across this room so hard my feet started hurting. I packed up everything I had in this room and left behind a few outfits. Once I was finished, I left and headed to Envy house.

Driving in the car blasting that, Mozzy. I can't lie, Dolla listened to him so much it rubbed off. Stopping at the store grabbing her some rellos. I grabbed her two boxes and she was definitely going to need them. I also grabbed a bottle of Remy.

When I arrived at her house her car was parked in the driveway. I used my key and let myself in. She had the music blasting and was in the kitchen. Envy was sitting at the table sacking up her dope and counting her money. Looking just like our mother from head to toe. Blunt hanging out her mouth as she focused. "Wassup big sis", she greeted me. "Hey baby sis", I leaned and kissed her on the cheek. Sitting across from her just watching. She had her gun right next to her and one laying on her lap. The money machine is on the table next to her. Money everywhere, and the scale right in front of her.

"Envy you looking just like momma", I smirked. "Man, momma didn't play did she", she smiled. A knock interrupted our conversation. She looked at Ma and slid the gun on the table over to me, while clutching the one on her lap. Slowly walking to the door guns pointed. "Who is it?", she yelled. "It's me Dolla fool, put the gun down and opened the door," he responded. I whispered, "Open the door but keep your gun out". She looked at me confused. Flinging the door open letting him in. He had some niggahs walk in before him. When he walked behind him, he grabbed the gun from Envy and smacked the dude in the back of the head. "What the fuck yo", she spazzed. "I know you got some rope and tape here", he looked at her. "In my trunk fool, what are you doing and why here", she continued spazzing. He ignored her. "So, I guess you didn't tell her yet," he said to me. "Tell me what", she asked? Dollah picked the dude up and carried him to the basement. He tied him up really good to a pole down there.

He came back to us in the kitchen. Envy lit her cigarette, probably racking her brain on what's going on. "Somebody better tell me what the fuck really going on. Why did y'all choose to bring a muthafuckah here, " she questioned. Dollah looked over at me and said, "Tell her". "TELL ME WHAT", she yelled! "Chill sis it's important", I told her. "Chill bitch you see what I'm doing right now and y'all choose to bring a muthafuckah to my real fucking house. Loyalty, we have places for this shit man", she scolled me. "Envy listen to me fuck them spots right now.

We can blow our cover", I tried calming her down. Dollah sat down and began rolling up his blunt. "Sis QC is trying to take us out. We have to figure out his plan", I explained to her. "I also think he is the one who killed momma", I told her. "What", she snapped. The look in her eyes turned cold. "What you mean he killed momma", she questioned? "We received some information from a guy named Know It All", I informed her. She sat down and rubbed her head. "So, all these years it was him I knew it", she started crying. I sat next to her and hugged her tight. "We're gonna get his ass don't worry", I whispered in her ear. "This muthafukah helped raise us and was momma's right-hand man," she cried. Dolla passes her the blunt when sitting down. "Please tell me you didn't have nothing to do with it," she asked him. "I knew he was crazy but no I swear I didn't know that" he told her. "I got your back though thru whatever I'm riding with you," he assured her. She hit that blunt so hard as the tears fell from her face. Envy hates embarrassment and will go to great measures to make you pay. I knew QC wanted to be trusted and I always told my mother I didn't like his ass. She swore up and down that he was a solid cat. He just gave me a snake like vibe. "So, who is the muthafuckah in the basement", she stood up. "That's this lil punk that's been doing secret runs for QC. I know he got some information," he told us. "Aww yea his ass is about to sing like a bird", Envy said.

Grabbing her gun and heading downstairs. We walked behind her, turning the lights off behind us. He was sitting there breathing hard as hell. I could hear his heart beating from where I was standing. Envy walked over and slapped his ass so hard with the barrel of her gun. Causing blood to fly out of his mouth onto the floor next to him. "Fuck y'all I don't owe you shit", he yelled. "Fuck us huh", I said. Punching him in the face a few times. "What the fuck I do to you", he muttered. Dollah walked over to us and stood in front of him. "You don't have much time so don't waste it on lies," he told him. "Tell you what I don't know shit," he mumbled. "I see we are going to be here a while, grab me a chair and two glasses of ice water Envy", I instructed. "Ok Dollah helped me clean this mess up the stairs' ', she said. Dollah followed but soon came back with the chair and water. "You got this real quick", he asked me? "Yea I got this", I assured him. Sitting the chair down in front of him. "You thirsty homeboy", I asked him. He nodded, yes. I took one of the glasses and drank it in front of him. "That was good", I smirked. "Now you tell me what I want to hear and I'll think about giving you a sip of this water", I told him. He sat there muggin me. "So, for starters what business do you have going on with QC ", I jumped right in. "Oh, you're not gonna say anything huh", I smacked his ass. "Now you go talk or you are gonna wish you would have in a few minutes". He started laughing. "What's so funny, muthafuckah", I asked? "For one y'all bitches don't scare me or that weak as fool Dollah ", he smirked.

"Chasity Dowers 1767 Lane. Drives a white BMW with

the plate reading "Momma Bear", Dollah said, walking down the stairs. Homie turned his head so quickly, focusing on Dollah. "You got a little brother and sister right about 8 and 10 years old. They attend Gerald R Ford if I'm not mistaken", Dollah continued. "Man, what the fuck keep my family out of this they have nothing to do with this", he pleaded. "Your family has everything to do with it", Envy said, joining us. Pulling out her gun and placing it against his head. I asked him again "What is your business with QC"? He sat in silence for a minute. "I'm not telling yall shit", he put his head down. "Do you not know I will shoot the fuck out of you and then head to your mother's house. Tell her the bad news and then kill everything moving in that house", I told him. "Sis, hand me the silencer", I told Envy. She handed it to me and I screwed it on the tip of the gun. Once I had it on, I shot him in the leg. "Ahhh", he screamed. "Now keep playing with me and I'll shoot you in every inch of your body", I warned him. He sat their crying. I was starting to get pissed the fuck off. Patients are growing very thin with his wanna be tough ass. "So, you are willing to let your family die just for QC someone who can care less about your ass. He is just using you", I told him. "I'm not saying shit", he gritted his teeth. "Ok cool" I smiled. "Envy lets go talk to his momma. Dollah kept an eye on him, I said. Dollah nodded in agreement. "You done fucked up boy trying to be tough", Dollah said to him.

Envy and I headed to the momma house. "So big sis, I

know you're cooking up a good ass plan right", she asked me. "Hell, yeah but it's definitely time to bring the savage out", I gripped the wheel. "We are gonna shut down the whole organization", I told her. "Yea he done fucked up now," she responded.

We eventually pulled up to his mother's house. It was a black and white with a black Jag in the driveway. "What's the plan Loyalty", she asked me? "We go in and shoot everyone in their sis", I cocked my gun. "Pull around the corner and I'll meet you there," I told her. Once I got out and tucked my gun I headed to the door. She pulled off to her destination. See this what I was afraid of. Muthafuckahs don't understand how to leave the evil me sleeping. Well, she may be woke for good now. I knocked on the door and a short older woman came to the door. The door flung open and she began cursing at me. "You better have a good damn reason why yo ass knocking on my door so late. "Yes, mam I have some important news concerning your son," I lied. "Is everything ok with him", she asked? Her tone changed up real quick she motioned me in. Soon as she shut the door, I pulled out the gun. "Yea your son told me to tell you he loves you", I smirked. I didn't even let her respond before I pulled the trigger. Watching her body drop to the ground made me think of my mother being shot down. It angered me even more but I couldn't pull myself to shoot his brother and sister. I snapped the picture and sent it to Dollah as I ran out into the dark. Fleeing to the car as my sister waited on me. Hoping in the car and she sped off quickly back towards the house. "I bet his ass talk now sis", I said to Envy. I showed her the picture in my phone. It's like sis drove faster just to see his reaction. "Was anybody else in the house," she asked me? "I think the kids but only she came to the door. I couldn't kill them sis not no babies", I told her. She nodded while turning the music up smoking her cigarette. I just sat back and got lost in my thoughts and the music. Momma always told us you get them before they get you. And make sure you get them all no matter who get caught in the way. You want a muthafuckah to talk you take away their heart and he'll sing your favorite tune. Before it's over, anybody that had anything to do with QC was dead to me. I'm not giving no passes to nan bitch ass wanna be. It's about to go down so hard they're gonna think my mother is reincarnated in the flesh. You called me back so let's play, QC ass was mine.

Pulling into the garage when we arrived back at Envy house. Once the door was all the way down, we got out of the car. Heading back downstairs to the basement. Dollah looked like had put a nice whoopin on him. He was sitting their head down as if he had been knocked out. Envy ran upstairs real quick. Coming back down with her water pitcher. "You showed him the picture yet," I asked Dollah.   "Naw I had knocked him out by then. Envy threw the picture of cold water on him. That woke his ass right up. "Fuck all y'all", he yelled. "You ready to talk now", Envy said to him. "I'm not saying shit to none of you bitches", he mugged her. He spit at her and missed. She backhanded him so hard. "Oh, so you not gone talk huh", I laughed. "Show his ass them pictures", I told Dollah. He looked up at the phone his face dropped. "What the fuck y'all on man. Bitch you killed my mother", he yelled! "Man fuck your momma now tell me what I need to know before I find out where your brothers at", Envy said. He cried so hard, but I can't feel bad now that our life depends on everything. "Ok Ok OK what do you want to know", he looked up broken. "Fuck, why my momma though", he cried. Dollah stepped up in front of him. "See you killed your momma being tough for the wrong person", he punched him. "So, what's the business that you have going on with QC", I stepped in? "He has me on lookout I was told to watch you and your sister movements. I report back to him with the details", he told us. "Watch us for what", I asked? "He just told me to keep an eye on y'all plus to kill the dude you met at the mall. Just last week he had me go and talk to this Cuban guy about you", he explained. "What". I kneeled down in from of him. "Yes, he told me to go deliver a message let the man know to be expecting some visitors. "So, you the one who tipped the Cuban in the Skee off", Dollah interrupted. "He is planning to take you two bitches and turn y'all hoes into dust," he laughed. Before I knew it, Envy blasted his ass. "Bam, Bam, Bam"! "Fuck all of them questions we found out what we needed to know. We now know that it's confirmed QC on bullshit so we need to focus on that, she explained.

I hate that I had to kill his mother but, in this game, you better pick the loyal side to be on. Ain't no sympathy in this here thing called life. But one thing for sure, two things for certain everybody is about to pay. "We gotta clean this up and get to work," I said. "Yea let's clean this shit up and go and figure out our next move," Dollah said.

Dollah went and disposed of the body while Envy and I cleaned up the basement. "Man, sis I can't believe all this shit", Envy spoke out. "I know sis I always knew that QC wasn't right," I sighed. "I never would have thought he had something to do with our momma's death", she continued. "Yea that tripped me out to be honest", I shook my head. It's always the ones you least expect to be a snake in the grass. The one beside you be the one pulling you down. Our mother schooled us so tough he had to know we would eventually find out. Thinking to myself, his ass has no mercy coming from me, period. "So, Envy, this is what we are going to do. I need an unrecognizable car. I'm going to pop this bitch off right. You will make sure it's a night y'all all in there. I will do a drive-by on the crib. Only after QC gets a mysterious call from someone threatening him. We are going to put a for sale sign in the trap house yard", I told her. "Sale the trap", she looked at me. "No not really sell it but make him think we are after I caused a scene about the shooting and you being there. You know QC the phone call is going to piss him off, to where he is talking shit to y'all about it, I explained. "Time to cause some friction in his bitch ass life but distract him from us for a minute so we can execute him and all his followers" Envy smirked. Once we finished, we waited on Dollah to call.

Chapter 8: I want him but can I trust him

After that night, all I could think about was the truth that got laid into our lap. How could this snake muthafuckah hold his composure all this time? What made him think that it was cool to think he could play us. My mother didn't raise no fool or no dummies. He had to have thought about revenge if we had ever found out. What I want to know is why the Cubans are looking for us. That is my next mission to figure it out. What is so important that they could want to be with us? What has QC gotten us into? Who will I have to kill to find out? Thoughts and questions filled my head. Sitting in my car outside the trap I continued to think. I decided to go out to my mother's old house and look around. Pulling off as QC was pulling up. The sight of his made my skin crawl but I had to play this shit right. Just riding past him as I made a U-turn not even making eye contact. He just looked and walked in the house, I watched from my rearview.

My mother's house was out on 52nd street right before you got to Baileys Grove. I turned into the driveway and parked the car. Stepping out, taking a deep breath as I looked around. I remember sitting on this porch with my sister and mother watching the stars. My momma was crazy but she didn't miss a beat while sharing some good moments. I was sitting beside her as she bounced Envy on her knee. "Girls I want y'all to know that your dreams can come true. It's about how bad you want them, she told us. No matter what we wanted to do she would have been cheering us on. I miss her so much and wish I could have saved her. I know one thing though; I will get revenge. No matter what it takes, I won't stop until everyone who had something to do with her death is dead. The loyalty I share with my mother no one can come between that.

Opening the door and walking slowly. Envy wasn't lying, everything was just the same. I began having flashbacks of us running through here as kids. Momma yelling doesn't break anything. Good times I swear. Also flashbacks of the night my mother walked out and never came back. I could feel the tears welled up in my eyes as my knees become weak. Dropping down to the floor I was so hurt and really upset. My mother was my everything and they took her from me. My sister and I didn't deserve that shit. The hurt was no longer an issue. It's the rage behind the situation that was ready to play.

First thing I did after collecting myself from the floor was go into my momma room. It was still the same besides the pallet on the floor. Someone was sleeping in here from the ashtray of put out blunts and a picture of momma and Envy, telling me my sister must come here often. I checked the closet to see if the safe was still under the floor. Just as I thought it was still here. I pulled it up out of the floor and it was a little heavy. Before sitting it down I noticed scratches on the floor as if someone was looking for this. They were looking in the wrong places. Envy was young but maybe she forgot exactly where it was at. Meaning she didn't remember the code to get in. I remembered it plain as day 0709129. I pressed in the numbers. The door clicked and it popped open. Pulling the door open to see what's been here this whole time. It had to be at least five hundred thousand dollars, a gold 357 magnum, two notebooks and a little diary. She had deeds, stocks, and investments. A phone, some diamonds. A few video tapes along with tape recordings. Taking the notebooks and tapes out and putting them into my backpack. I also took a couple stacks of money out. Closing the safe and putting it back into the floor. Making sure I left no trace to where it was. It may not be Envy staying here. She would have said something to me about trying to find the safe. Or maybe she has been here and on some funny shit with QC. So many thoughts went through my head. Walking around the house checking all momma's old spots to see money was still where she left it. This house had over a million dollars stashed here, that's why we never sold her property.

My phone began to ring. I searched my purse for it, but by the time I found it the ringing stopped. Checking the missed call, it was Envy. I called her right back and she answered quickly. "Wassup sis where you at?", she asked me? "Headed to find some shit for tonight," I responded. "Ok bet I have everything in play. I told QC we needed a meeting about some shit I've been hearing about someone making a move on us. Once we are all in the room, I'll text you a sentence. That's when you will make the call to QC, then pull the drive-by, she explained. "Word, I got you sis let's make his ass sweat then", I said. We hung up. I didn't tell her about me getting in the safe until I went through this shit I took out.

I called up Dollah to see if he had the car for me tonight. "Wassup Loyalty", he answered. "Hey, did you take care of that for me," I asked him? "Yea everything is good and ready to go," he responded. "Great, can you meet me real quick at Envy's crib", I asked? "Yes, I can do everything ok", he asked? "Yea just meet me ok", I said seductively. Envy made a run to Detroit so I had little time for playing. It's been a while since Dollah and I messed around. We have been so busy we haven't had the time to link again. It was something about him that drove me crazy and I yearned for it from time to time. I knew once all this was over, I would be with him. He sounded a little busy so I knew I would beat him there.

Arriving in Envy as I knew I would get there before him. I went in and showered, changing into something sexy. After getting out of the shower I looked out the window and saw him pulling in. The guest room showed the entire driveway. Not soon after I heard him using the key to come in. I laid on the bed and waited. "Yo Loyalty wassup", he called out. "Up here I need your help," I yelled back. Shortly after he opened the door, walking and standing so perfectly. He was wearing a red Jordan shirt with the matching basketball shorts. His black durag set it off. He stared at me with those brown eyes. "I need you", I said, licking my lips. "Oh, so you need me huh", he smiled. "How may I help you baby", he smirked at me. "Come here, let me show you," I said. As he walked over to me, he began stripping out of his clothes. By the time he climbed in the bed all he was wearing was his boxers. Dick hard as a rock. I couldn't blame him because I was so wet thinking of what was about to happen. Laying on top of me kissing me with those soft supple lips. Caressing my body as he held me tightly. Giving me butterflies as he ran his soft hands down my back. Moaning softly as he began to suck on my nipples. He makes my body feel so good. "Why did you wait so long for me to touch you this way," he whispered in my ear? "I'm here now, that's all that matters," I told him. Spreading my legs as he made his way down my torso. Placing his warm soft tongue onto my clit. Causing me to take a deep breath as I gripped his head. Wrapping my legs around his shoulders as he licked and slurped my juices. I don't know what he was doing to me but I never wanted him to stop. My legs started shaking, something terrible. I let out a loud moan as I came. Holding my breath as he kept going. Soon gasping so deep as he put his third leg inside my wetness. Going in and out slowly and gently. Closing my eyes and biting my lip as he stroked and I scratched his back. This man was turning me on and out in so many ways. I've never felt this way before about any man. The moment he saved my life played back in my head, causing me to get wetter. From the sound of his moans let me know he was truly enjoying me as well. "Let me get on top," I whispered in his ear. He turned over, holding me in place so he did not slip out of me. Something about the way we turned caused him to go deeper. That took the cake. I placed my hand on his chest as he gripped my thighs. I began grinding up and down slowly at first. He grinded in motion with me as I rode him. He felt so good inside me I swear. Little did he know he was mine forever. Before I could climax, he flipped me over and began to hit it from the back. Thrusting faster and deeper inside me caused me to moan louder. He wrapped my hair around his hand pulling my hair as he slapped my ass. Still thrusting so deeply. "Oh my God", I was able to eventually say. "Tell me your mine," he mumbled, biting his lip. It was hard to get it out in between his deep strokes but I did. "I'm Yours", I cried out. I meant that shit so he had officially written his name in it. He then grabbed my waist with both hands going deeper and faster. Causing the bed to rock and hit the wall loudly. I moaned out in between deep breaths. Trying not to run as I took every stroke while biting the sheets. He was working my ass out, you hear me. Digging inside me like he had a point to prove. I can tell by his motions, showed me he was about to blow soon. Holding me tighter and moving faster. Before I knew it, he pushed so deep and stayed there. Moving very little with his eyes closed tight and his legs shaking. "Ohhh shiiitt", he moaned. As he busted inside me collapsing onto my back. We both laid there trying to catch our breath. "Loyalty baby you meant that right", he broke the silence. "Did I mean what?", I asked. "That you were mine. "he looked at me. I looked him in the eye and responded. "Yes, I can be yours if you promise to not hurt me", I said. "I won't hurt you ever", he kissed me. "Dollah, I want to be with you but I'm not ready for a committed relationship until business is handled", I explained to him. "Come here", he pulled me close. I laid in his arms rubbing his chest. "We are gonna handle this together and then we are gonna leave together," he assured me. I told him about the safe and what I took out. He told me we can go over it later and that he wanted me to go finish the drops with him. We dressed and I headed out with him. Envy should be back soon so we can put the plan in effect. As we were riding, I explained the plan to Dollah so he wouldn't be shocked at the meeting Envy called. "So, what are you going to do when he wonders why you are not there too," he asked? "You will come up with something, he will believe it because he knows I'm rebellious", I answered. "Dollah pull over please," I insisted. He did just as I asked. "Wassup you good", he looked concerned. "Are you really on our side or are you a part of QC bullshit too", I seriously asked him? Looking him in the eyes not blinking once. I need to know this and his eyes will tell it all. I would hate to have to kill him one day but if he is on that side of the fence, he's dead. "Loyalty, I told you I have nothing to do with no secret operation. Even though we are growing a deep bond I don't want to hurt you. I would never hurt Envy. Yes, I grew up under QC and have loyalty to him but that doesn't mean I agree with what he is doing. For some reason, he is changing and on some bs. That shit tripped me out. If I wanted to kill you or your sister, I wouldn't have built a bond first. That's a waste of time if I have to kill you. I stay away from you so the ties we have don't cloud my judgment. The respect I have for your mother is deep. It's my honor to help y'all turn some shit up", he broke down to me. He didn't blink once either as he stared me in the eyes while talking. "Trust me, Loyalty please," he pleaded. "You have to trust me as well Dollah," I responded. "We have to trust each other and handle our business. I got y'all back to the T, " he continued. Leaning over and kissing me so passionately. "Well in that case let's go get our empire", I said sitting back in my seat.

The three of us were fierce and not to be fucked with. This city had no idea of the storm about to come through. Once all these bitches are gone, we will run this empire as if my mother had never left. The streets have been quiet with her gone, now was time for her daughters to wake up. Looking out the window mugging just thinking how QC had it coming.

8.

Make Him Sweat A little Bit

So, Envy met with me behind the Agave restaurant to change cars. She had gotten me a car to do the drive-by. She told me to wait here until she called to text me that everyone was there. The meeting was going to start soon and I needed someone to call QC when I was ready. I sat there for about forty-five minutes till she texted me. I saw a crackhead asking for change outside the liquor store across the street. So, I pulled over there and told him I'll give him a hundred dollars to call this man and say this. Handing him the paper with what to say. He was so happy about the hundred he was ready. I dialed a private QC number. He didn't answer the first time so I called back and he did. Man, that crackhead went the fuck off and hung up on him. I paid him and pulled off. That was easy. Envy left me a 40 under the seat, she said. When I got to the corner, I pulled the skull cap over my face and placed my black gloves on. Grabbing the gun from under the seat. I pulled in front of the house after texting my sister. It's a go. Leaving the car running as I stood in the front of the house. I began shooting that damn house the fuck up. Some lil dude ran from the back and busted back.

His mistake I popped his dumb ass too. I emptied the clip, jumped in the car, and sped off. I drove to the destination spot where Dollah texted me. He told me to look for the white guy in the Infiniti truck.

When I got there, he was parked on a ramp downtown by the JW Marriott on the top level. He was to get rid of the car I was in and I was to take the car he was driving. "So where are you taking it", I asked? "I'll take the car to my garage and dismantle the entire thing," he told me. "Ok cool Dollah told me to text him once I was with you," I informed him. I texted him to let him know the car was in his possession. "He told me to tell you he will meet you at the spot in an hour", I explained to him. I jumped into the truck and pulled off. Stopping by the room to shower and clean myself up. I kept the gun though; this is definitely all mine. I've always had a thing for them in their forties.

Once I cleaned myself up, I drove over to the trap house and watched QC lose his head. When I pulled up, they were all outside on the porch. I had to get my act ready. Getting out of the car to ambulance and police. Then EMTs were picking up the lil dude I popped, he took one to the chest and one in the leg. I walked up to the two dudes on the porch. "What the fuck happened here", I asked them? "Somebody came through and sprayed this bitch up," one said. "Yea QC was hit in the shoulder," the other said. "What?", I acted shocked. "Yea he is good though he is in his office talking to the police". "Where is my sister," I asked? "She is there too and Dollah", he told me. Standing out front looking around until the officers were done inside. I walked in as the officers were walking out.

When I got in my sister was sitting in the front room with a bandage on her arm. I rushed over to her I hope I didn't shoot my sister. "Sis you good", I asked? She gave me a little smirk. "I'm good sis I got grazed nothing major though", she told me. "Where is Dollah", at I said to her. "He in there with QC, he got hit in the shoulder", she told me. I walked towards the back room. Got my game face on and busted thru the door. "What the fuck is going on here and how did my sister get shot", I yelled. "Somebody hit us up", Dolla answered. "Who the fuck would do that shit QC", I turned to him. "Look not right now with your dramatic shit Loyalty", he responded. "What the fuk you mean my sister get shot and you say not right now", I continued. 'Your sister is fine she got grazed hell I'm the one who got shot, " he mugged me. Before I said anything someone came in and interpreted us. "Lil G didn't make it he passed on the way to the hospital", the guy told QC. "See this is why I'm selling this fucking place. You talking about my sister got shit going crazy from the looks of it you the one with the heat", I leaned over his desk. "You not selling shit lil girl who the fuck you think you are", he stood up. "I'm the motherfucker who own this house and you fucked up and put my sister in danger", I stared his ass down. "You need to be worried about finding out who the fuck bringing heat your way not this house", I yelled.

"Don't worry about that I'll find out who the fuck did this hoe shit", he sat back down. "Well, you heard what I said I'm selling this house period and taking my sister out of here", I told him. Trying not to laugh in his face every time he grabs his arm. Wish I would have bust his ass in his head. "You heard what I said Loyalty", he turned his back. Soon as he did that, I started reaching in my purse to grab my gun. Before I can get to it Dollah grabbed me. "Come on, let's go check on Envy," he insisted. We walked out the room into the living room. "Yo Dollah can you take me to make a little run real quick," Envy said to him. "Yea bet let's go then I'll buy y'all some food or something," he smirked.

We ended up going to Wing Heaven where his homeboy Mook worked. Dollah and Mook were thick as thieves since childhood. Mook came from the streets but he didn't stay in the streets. He told us that we would be able to eat and talk in peace.

Dollah made a right off Burton onto Eastern. He turned around into the post office parking lot to park in front of the restaurant. We sat for a minute and Envy was smoking the L she rolled up. "How's your arm sis?", I asked her. "I'm good sis, just glad it was only a graze," she smirked. "I'm so sorry sis you know it wasn't on purpose," I assured her. Thinking to myself on how did she even get hit in the first place. When she texted, me she told me that she was in a good position to not get hit. After they finished smoking, we headed in. No one but Mook was and they were closing soon. Dollah ordered our food and then joined us at the table.

(QC)

Sitting in my office wreaking my brain on who the fuck had the heart to go against me. Let alone shoot up one of my spots. I know damn well the Cubans ain't that crazy. Pouring me a shot as I waited on Know It All to call back. He's gotta know something, his ass better know something. Rocking in my chair rubbing my shoulder. Soon as I thought shit was bad, my phone rang. Someone had killed my lil homie mother and he is missing. I slammed the phone down onto the desk. What the fuck is really going on. I need to figure this shit out, take these bitches out and execute my plan. So much was going through my mind. Sometimes I do miss how Lady kept everything together. But I had to get rid of her ass because she was starting to only think for herself and them damn kids of hers. She never loved me like I loved her and that's what got her ass killed. I cannot let their daughters find this shit out. I knew I had Envy just where I wanted her wild ass too. Wonder what Loyalty ass gone do when she find out I fuck the shit out if her sister every chance I get. Opening my drawer and dumping the bag of coke on the desk. Taking one big hit, my arm was killing me. Know It All better hit me back before I pay his ass an unpleasant visit. It's war time and I will come out on top. Take another hit and lean back into my chair.

(Loyalty)

After eating we dropped Envy off to her car at home. She insisted on making a few moves. I told her we will link up later to make our next move on QC. Something wasn't right, she was acting weird as hell after a text she received. Maybe it's her so-called boyfriend she claims to have but won't bring around. Dolla and I had a few drops to make as well as pickups. We pulled off from Envy house and got to work. "Loyalty you ok", Dolla broke my train of thought. "Yea I'm good it's just Envy acting real weird", I said. "Yea I honestly thought the same thing honestly. She got grazed trying to shield QC, he told me. "WHAT"!! "Yeah, it was weird though because after she got your text, she moved closer to him as if she wanted to be shot," he explained. "I don't know what she is going through but you need to talk to your sister soon," he assured me. "Oh, I'm definitely going to find out what's her problem frfr" I told him. I stared out the window as we rode down Kalamazoo.

Dollah ran into Tuffy on Kalamazoo and 44th to grab some shit. He returned to the car ten minutes later carrying two duffle bags. I popped the trunk for him. When he was back in the car and pulling off, I spoke up. "I think we should hit all the QC trap spots he is running. "When we take over, I don't want no one he so called raised in my organization but you" I informed him. "If that's how you wanna play it you know I'm rocking" he smirked. "I need a list of every pickup spot and drop off location by tomorrow," I told him. He nodded in agreement.

(Envy)

My mind was racing. I had to come home and get my head right. What the fuck was I thinking jumping in front of QC, snake MF killed my mother. I can't believe after all the shit he has ever said to me was a lie. How could you look me in the eye and say you love me but killed the woman who created me. Loyalty is going to flip the script when she finds out that I've been sleeping with QC since momma died. He has let me down on all levels. I knew he was up to something the day Loyalty arrived but I can't figure out what. My heart was broken so badly these last few days. I haven't even told him that I'm pregnant. Between him and Spooks was the father. Spooks is my boyfriend on the low. QC hates that. He caught us at the strip club that night. I lied and told my sister it was a shootout. I'm scared to tell my sister because I don't think she is going to take this well. I don't want to kill him but he must go and I must never tell who the father of my child is. I hate keeping secrets from my sister but the time to tell her is not now. Especially when war is her state of mind. I sat back on the couch trying to stay calm. Since my mom was killed, I suffered from bad anxiety. When I get overwhelmed, I can have a panic attack and it triggers my asthma. We needed to contact them Cubans asap as well but who can get us a meeting. It was racking my brain on who to call. It came to me; I was going to have to go see QC. He has a few numbers in his phone I needed and I knew just how to get them. Going to my room and packing me an overnight bag. Placing some sexy pjs and an outfit for tomorrow morning. I texted him and told him I'm alone and needed to see him. He told me to meet him at his house. I jumped in the shower and put on my lavender baby oil. Slipped on my black heels and long black trench. My dark Gucci glasses I decided to let my hair down under my black hat. Spraying the perfume that he bought me, as I walked out of my room. Heading out my door, locking it behind me. It was only gonna take me about fifteen minutes to get to his spot. I stopped at the liquor store and grabbed a fifth of Patron and some swishers.

When I made it there, he was pulling in at the same time. Pulling into the garage behind him. I would park in his garage so if anybody was to call themselves snooping, they wouldn't see my car. Walking into the house behind him. "How's your arm baby," I asked him? "It hurts but you know I'm good," he responded. Sitting down in the living room. "Well, I got us a drink baby let's chill", I smiled at him. Trying not to show him how upset I was with him. "Whew baby hold that thought I have to pee", I spoke up. Carry all my belongings with me just in case he gets the urge to snoop. Ok Envy pull it together you got this. I peppered myself in the mirror. "Yo Envy you good", I heard him yell. "Yea baby here I come", I yelled back, flushing the toilet. Walking out after washing my hands keeps them a lil wet to play it off. QC pays a great deal to shit and one slip up will tip him off.

We took some shots together, after my first two I pretended to drink by no longer using the shot glass. But faking to sip from the bottles. Watch him get fucked up alone. His dumb ass didn't even notice that he was drinking alone. "Baby ain't you hot in that coat"? he asked me. What he didn't know was that I was completely naked under this coat. "Yes, baby these shots are getting me warm", I smirked. I stood up and dropped the jacket to the floor revealing my sexy naked body. QC evil ass was so attractive for his age though. He had the body of a very healthy thirty-year-old man. You wouldn't dare think he was forty-five years old. The way she put it down in the bedroom was amazing. I don't know how I got myself emotionally involved in him. "Envy what your sister is up to with selling these houses, you're trying to leave me," he mentioned. "She is not going to sell the house I think she is just trying to piss you off as usual", I kissed his neck as I sat on his lap. After I took my last hit of the bottle, I dropped a sleeping pill in the bottle. So, after I put this good, good on him I knew for a fact he had gone to sleep good. I started grinding on him slowly faking like I was still drinking. The pushing the bottle to his lips watching him take a few big sips. I felt his dick getting hard as he enjoyed rubbing my body. "We need to get Envy out of the picture for good"., he mumbled. "Whatever you want baby"! I whispered in his ear. Soon pulling his hard dick out and began to give him head. I don't know what's going to be more pleasurable. The way I'm about to put it on him or the day I put a bullet in his fuckin head.

Meanwhile I can't lie, he definitely put it down on me. Just as I expected, though his ass passed out right after. As soon as I knew he was dead, I grabbed his phone. Plugging his first phone into my iPad. He had another phone somewhere in one of his pockets. I made sure to get that one too. My homeboy Sony taught me how to hack phones in a matter of seconds. As I put everything back in place once I finished my phone rang. It was Loyalty. After a few rings, I answered it. "Hello"! I picked up. "Hey sis where are you at we need to talk," she said. "I'm a little busy right now, can I call you back," I replied. "Envy whatever you are doing can wait sis for real to meet me in a half-hour," she snapped. "Look Loyalty I'll get with you first thing in the morning," I told her before hanging up.

Soon as I hung up and turned around QC was waking up. "Who are you talking to?", he asked me. "Oh baby, that was my sister's annoying ass", I said quickly. "Come lay with me E", he told me. I went and laid with him. "QC we have to stop this when Loyalty finds out she is gonna flip out", I looked at him. "I told you, don't worry about that I got a plan for her if you are really gonna roll with me", he smirked. The look on his face told it all of the plans he is thinking. "What do you mean by the plan for her", I asked. I was trying so hard not to get upset. "Do you love me E and don't you want to be my queen"? he went on. "Yes, I do love you and I thought I was already your queen", I said. "Well show me you mean it and kill her", he sat up. I sat there speechless, he wanted me to kill my sister.

"Kill my sister"! I repeated. "Yes, that way I'll know for sure you are not trying to roll on me or hurt me. I'll know for sure that you are down with me for sure.

9.

Let's Talk Sis

I got up at about nine this morning, showered and got dressed. Dollah was still asleep. I ended up staying the night with him since Envy's ass was bullshitting. I just wanted to see what she came up with on how to get into QC's phone. Her ass has been acting weird since the other day. She is always up to something or laid up. I also wanted to talk to her about momma's house. We need to figure out who is going there. Also, when, and why, what the fuck are they looking for.

Just as I was about to call her ass, she texted me and said meet her at the Cracker Barrel for breakfast. Luckily, I'm hungry. I agreed to meet her in thirty minutes. I grabbed my purse and headed out to meet her. We really needed to get some shit out on the floor. I don't know why I came home too but I damn sure am about to get to the bottom of this shit. I know one thing she better be playing for the right side.

I waited about fifteen minutes and she came walking in. Sliding into the booth sitting across from me. "Wassup Loyalty", she greeted me! "Hey sis how are you today", I responded? "You know me high as the Himalayas," she laughed. "Well, that's good to hear," I smirked. I didn't waste any time after we ordered our food to get right to it. "So, Envy what was going on before I got here", I asked? "What do you mean Loyalty", she questioned back. "I'm saying why did QC say I have to come back", I continued. "Hell, if I know I found out you were coming, what the day before. That's why all this here to watch me shit was so damn amusing to me, " she told me. "I don't get what was so important for me to be here doing this shit," I said. "Look Loyalty I don't know what the purpose is for you being here. Right questions but wrong person you asking", she stated. My mother used to say that a lot. That was her way of saying basically you were talking to the wrong muthafuckah. "Envy have you been out to momma house", I asked her? "I stopped by not too long ago. I go out there sometimes. Just smoke and think really", she explained. "I go out there, lay in momma's room, smoke my brains out and look at our picture", she went on. "Well, have you been looking for her safe", I asked? "No, I don't, I know exactly where that safe is. Just can't remember the code", she sighed. "I know the code to it", I said sipping my coffee. "Good I don't need it but I knew you had it so I never tripped. This would be the time I should tell her that the code is engraved into our lockets momma gave us. Should I tell her about the scrapes on the floors? Is she telling me the truth? So many questions crossed my mind in the moment. I know she is my baby sister and our bond deeper than the streets. I also know money and power can truly change a person. I just hope it didn't change my sister.

"Look Loyalty, what's going on? Why are you asking me about momma's house and her safety?" she mugged me. "I'm just asking because I went there and wanted to know how it has been going. I could tell someone comes and goes out there", I explained to her. "Envy can I trust you", just blurted out my mouth. I was thinking about it and spoke too soon. All hell broke loose. "What the fuck did you just ask me", she frowned. I sat there trying to gather my thoughts. "Loyalty what the fuck did you just ask me", she repeated herself. The anger was written all over her face.: I didn't mean it like that, I spoke up. Nawwww yes you did", she started gathering her things. "Envy please listen", I said. "Fuck that bitch you listen", she said pointing her finger in my face. "Bitch you got me all the way fucked up. Day in and day out loyalty to this fucking game has given me a run for my money. Someday all the money I make can't purchase the time I invested here in the bullshit. You got some fucking nerve college girl to question that", she snapped off. "Envy", I said trying to get a word in. "You know what Loyalty fuck you and don't talk to me until you get the fucking answers you're looking for ", she stood up. "Envy wait listen I'm sorry", I spoke out. "You listen Loyalty I don't need your fucking apologies or I don't need you around me if your gonna question my loyalty", she said, slamming her money on the table. Grabbing her purse and headed out. Leaving me there looking stupid as hell. I was not expecting her to flip out and leave. I paid for our food and headed to my car.

When I got into the car she was long gone. I tried calling her but just as I expected she didn't answer. Sitting there resting my head on the steering wheel. Deciding to ride by her house and see if she was there. Just as I thought her car was pulled into the driveway. I pulled in behind her, not getting away from me now. Walking into the house to find her in the kitchen smoking and counting her money. I grabbed the chair across from her sitting down. "Didn't ya momma tell you to speak when you enter a room", she looked up at me. "Envy, listen to me. I don't want to fight," I told her. "Well why are you throwing blows my way then," she smirked. "I'm just trying to figure shit out sis. I stepped into "I don't know what, how do you expect me to think "I stared at her. "For one, don't come here thinking you are my momma. We are a team we equal Loyalty, ain't no leaders in between each other, " she said hitting her blunt. "You don't fucking own me or can't tell me what the hell to do". "I'm not trying to be your momma. Don't get it twisted though I am the leader in this shit. I'm your big sister and I will always be all up in your shit and that's facts", I stood up. "Fuck you", she said standing up. Before I knew it, I fired on her ass dead in her face. She swung back quickly and caught me in the jaw. We flipped the table over and went tumbling down with it. Tussling, pulling hair, and swinging. I managed to get on top of her grabbing her arms. "You feel better now", I held her down. "Get the fuck off me", squirmed. "Envy calm the fuck down for real and talk to me", I pleaded. "Let me go", she yelled! "Not till you agree to talk to me", I continued to hold her. "You're my sister and I love you no matter what", I began to cry. She was so pissed. I knew I was wrong for hitting her but she has been wanting to fight for years. I knew she would never hit me first though. We both knew that she couldn't beat me. My sister is crazy though and I really don't want to fight her like this. "Envy calm the fuck down and talk to me", I said. "OK now get the fuck off me', she said gritting her teeth. "I'll get up if you're gonna be calm," I said. I took a deep breath and let her up. The look she was giving me assured me she wasn't going to attack. Soon as we were up on our feet, she punched me dead in the eye. "Don't ever put your hands on me again," she mugged me. My shit was hurting so bad. I didn't swing back because our next step was not worth it. "Ok you owe me that", I said. Walking into the living room, holding my eye, sitting on the couch. She eventually came in and sat down. "Look Loyalty I'm with you all the way sis. I don't need all the pressure though "she sighed. "Envy I'm not trying to add pressure on your back. I want the MF that killed our mother to pay", I said. "Well, we want the same thing so get off my fucking back", she stated. I just sat there and watched her light her blunt. "What Loyalty", she looked at me? I grabbed her blunt and hit it so hard. Took me back to my first-time smoking with her ass. She's been smoking for a long time. I love the smell but never really got into it. Plus, my mother was on my case so hard I didn't get to do much. Count money, practice with guns, and take care of my sister. I never had a chance. Well not until I got to college. Look at me now back here and about to cause hell around this bitch. I want revenge and I'm not stopping till I get it.

We sat there smoking in silence for about an hour. Not saying a word to each other. Until Envy broke the silence. "So, what's the plan Loyalty", she asked? "We need to get a hold of them Cubans and get them on our side. Find out exactly what QC did and why he killed our mother", I responded. "Well, I got this, maybe we can get some answers out of it", she said. Placing a tablet in front of me. "What's that?", I asked. "I was able to copy all of the QC information into my tablet. We now have access to all his contacts", she said. "How the hell did you get him to let those phones out of his sight?", I questioned her. "That's not important as long as we got it," she smirked. Envy's phone started ringing. It was QC ass yelling about something. "I have to make a move sis I'll be back in a minute," she said. "Let me look through this and I'll see what I can find while you're gone", I told her. She headed out to see what he wanted.

I sat here wondering what was up with my sister. She seems very irritated lately. I don't want her to think that I'm against her because I'm not. She gotta remember I've been gone, I just got dropped in the middle. All these new people, QC secretly turned against us, the Cubans after us. I mean what the fuck is really going on. Then to top it off we set some shit up and you try to shield this fool. QC may have something to do with our mothers death. I've only been here a few months and have killed five people so I deserve to know everything. Why must I be left in the dark in the midst of the storm? I know I'm tired of playing games. I'm ready to go to war with everyone. I don't give a fuck about who get caught in the crossfire. The Demon inside me is awake and I'm ready for whatever. Whoever had anything to do with my mother's death is dead. I want blood by any means necessary. I just sat here on the couch thinking. Lighting the blunt Envy left in the ashtray. I'm not moving till her ass gets back. We need to figure shit out and get a plan in motion. It's time to lock and load. Leaning back on the couch as I took a hit of the blunt.

We needed a rock-solid plan to get to his ass. I wanted him dead so bad I could taste it. My phone began to ring. It was Dolla. "Hello", I answered. "Wassup Loyalty, where are you at? I need to holla at you", he told me. "I'm at Envy crib", I told him. "Ok I'm headed your way is Envy there", he asked. "Naw she left about twenty minutes ago", I replied.

I continued smoking till he got there. He didn't waste any time he got here about ten minutes later. Walking in and joining me on the couch. "You smoking now", he asked? "Don't judge me ok", I smirked. He grabbed the blunt and hit it. "Good you relaxed cuz I'm about to fuck ya mood up", he shook his head. "Wassup", I said. "Well, I went and hollered at Know It All. He told me some shit that fucked me up", he said. "What he say", I said concerned. "Well one thing is he was able to get a number to some too rank Cuban dude. He has agreed to meet with you and Envy alone", he handed me the paper. "Ok and what else is up Dollah". "Word is Envy might be pregnant and it's between two niggahs". "What", I was shocked! "Yea but you won't believe me when I tell you who", he sat back. Thinking to myself if I was ready for the information. "Who Dolla", I asked? "Spooks and QC", he told me. "QC", I repeated. "Yea man I guess they got something going on", he went on. I didn't know what to say or who to be more mad at. Envy for not telling me shit or QC for fucking my lil sister. All I know is I was furious with shit I just heard. "You sure QC might be a possibility", I palmed my face. "Yes, apparently it's been going on for a lil minute. That's why QC was so mad about her and Spooks getting closer. I knew she was fucking with Spooks but QC I never suspected", he explained to me.

I was furious as hell right now just thinking of his old ass fucking my baby sister. Knowing damn well he was playing with her heart. First you harm my mother, then you take advantage of my sister. "He must die Dollah", I said. He began rolling up another blunt. "He was definitely going to get his", he responded. "We just need to find out what side Envy is really rocking on", he said.

"You're right because if she plans to stand in my way, she gotta go with her bitch ass lover. My mother's death will be revenged", I said. "Envy on our side I think naw I know she is. She is just torn between the two, especially if she been fucking with him like that", Dollah said. "Well, I'm definitely going to find the fuck out and she will be choosing, and QC will be dying", I insisted.

After we smoked, he told me he had a few runs to make and will be hitting me up soon with a meeting time and location with the Cuban. This weed had me so high all I could do was laugh at myself. I decided to take a ride to visit my momma. I hadn't been to the cemetery in a while and this was more than a reason to go. Tears filled my eyes as I drove headed that way. Just thinking about why I went off to college and left my baby sister alone. I pulled up to the cemetery and was parked over by my mother. Walking over to her grave gave me chills. Tears just streamed down my cheek. When I approached her plot, I dropped to my knees crying so hard. Momma I'm so sorry that I let you down. I was supposed to protect Envy and look out for her. I never thought that QC would have gotten to her like that momma. I can't believe he deceived us like this momma. You put so much trust into that man over the years. He has another thing coming if he really thinks he is gonna win against me.

10.

Pick A Side And Pick It Now (QC)

Sitting behind my desk furious. I was ready to start shutting shit down. I called Envy and told her to get her ass here she needs to pick a side. Lighting my cigarette waiting. She finally walked her ass in here and sat down. "Wassup, you rang", she said sitting down. "We need to start making moves so you need to start cutting corners", I told her. "What do you mean start cutting corners", she frowned. "Just like I said we need to kill everyone including your fucking sister", I got straight to it. She just stood there silent for a minute. "She won't be the first to go but she will be going, you hear me Envy", I said. "I'm not killing my sister QC", she folded her arms. I stood up so fast and pulled my gun from my waist, putting it towards her head. "You either with me or against me", I whispered in her ear. "If you don't get that gun away from my damn head you better shoot me now," she mugged me. Envy had the heart of a lion and wasn't scared at all. That's what I liked so much about her crazy ass. Soon as I pulled the gun down from her head, she attacked me. Giving me the meanest hit to the face with a razor. "Bitch you cut me", I said grabbing my face. She pushed me back into my chair holding the blade to my neck. "Don't you ever in your fucking life pull a gun on me", she cried. "You knew I wasn't going to shoot you baby", I looked at her. "I don't know shit just don't you ever do that shit again you hear me", she threw me a towel. I was so pissed and wanted to shoot her ass now for real but I just couldn't do it. I grabbed the duffel bag next to me and threw it at her. "Take this and get the fuck out", I yelled. "Make sure you break it all down and call me when you're done", I informed her. She stormed out slamming the door behind her. Little did she know that all this just showed me whose side she was on and I'll have to kill her ass too. Sitting down lighting my blunt. I have to think of a plan to get their ass. I can't believe it all came down to this, but hey when it comes to that paper, I let nothing get in the way.

II.

It's On Now

I just couldn't stomach the fact that this MF wanted me to kill my own sister. He has lost his damn mind. Heaven or hell my mother will get my ass for going against the grain. I have to come clean to Loyalty and tell her everything. She is going to flip the fuck out but at least she'll know the truth. On top of being pregnant, she won't kill me. I wasn't scared of shit but my sister. Loyalty was not to be fucked with especially when she feels crossed. They say I'm a reflection of my mother. What they don't know is my sister has the savage in her my mother was. Sitting in my car thinking, when I noticed the blood on my shirt from me cutting QC ass. I headed home. I have to shower and collect my thoughts fast.

Standing in the shower mind is racing so fast. QC has lost his complete mind thinking I'm going to kill my own sister. My mother will haunt me for the rest of my life. I can't believe I'm pregnant, so many thoughts crossed my mind. I just need to take a ride and talk to my mother. I haven't been to the cemetery in a long time. I know she is probably very upset with me. After getting dressed I texted Loyalty and told her to meet me at momma's house tonight. I also told her we needed to talk alone. She texted me back and told me she agreed.

Rolling through the streets so frustrated with all that is going on around me. I'm really just ready to send this whole damn city up in flames. First someone kills my mother, then this muthafukah wanna turn against us, as well as fuk my lil sister. When I say I'm just ready to walk right up to him and blow his brains out. Even though I knew that wouldn't be smart, I'm just over his ass all together. Hell, whoever wants to go with him can die honestly. I couldn't wait to hear what Envy had to say either. After the text she sent to me she must feel my heated vibe. I really was shocked at what Dollah had to say and it pissed me off.

On my way home I got a call from a homie from back in the day. I noticed it was my homie Uni aka Sugar. Don't get it twisted though there wasn't anything sweet about her crazy ass. When we were kids, she and I grew up together. She left when we got about sixteen or seventeen. I heard she was back and opened a car wash or some shit but didn't expect her to be looking for me. "Wassup ", I answered the phone. "Wassup bitch", she replied. "Long time no hear from strangers ", I continued. "Well yea last I heard you were in college. But now I hear you out here causing havoc ", she said. "Don't believe everything you hear", I told her. "C'mon now I know you and how you move so wassup Loyalty", she quickly replied. "I don't know who your source is but tell them spit facts and not rumors. Now tell me what I owe for the courtesy call Sugah". "Word on the street is that we need to meet up and talk", she insisted. "Oh well in that case meet me at Garfield. I can be there in about ten minutes", I told her. "Bet see you then", she hung up. My day just keeps getting more interesting by the second. I head en route to Garfield Park. As I rode down Burton crossing Breton, all I could think about was Envy and how she laid with the man who may have taken part in our mothers death. As bad as she wanted to get the person behind and now it may have been her lover. I know she is furious as hell but Envy's ass has gone too far. No way in hell should have slept with his old ass. Snake muthafuka I can't wait to put these hollow tips in his damn head. Right idea but wrong damn sisters. My blood was boiling and I wasn't going to rest until I put this niggah down. On the other hand, what could Sugah want with me? At the light on Burton and Kalamazoo I reached into the glove department and grabbed my gun. Checking the click to make sure it was fully loaded and ready to blow. I was on tip with everybody and wasn't going to get caught slippin. She was my dawg and all back then but just like the weather and time people change too. Taking it off slowly and sliding it under my jacket into my shorts.

    I pulled up to the park and there were about three cars parked in the lot. Backed into the spot closest to the bathrooms. Texted the number she called from telling her I was here. About five minutes later the door to the

Denali truck flew open. She hops out of the back and proceeds to my car. I unlocked the door for her to hop right in. "Wassup Sugah", I greeted her. "Hey college girl", she smirked. "Yea ok", I laughed.

She leaned against the door turning to face me, so I did the same giving her my full attention. She looked down at the gun on my lap with a smirk on her face. "You planning on shooting me or something", she asked. "Honestly that depends on this conversation Sugah". "Damn it's like that now", she frowned. "Well just to let you know if you do shoot me, I doubt you make it out this park", she laughed. Looking at her with one eyebrow raised thinking to myself "yea ok". "Sugah right now it's so much going on I don't know who to trust", I told her. "Well Loyalty I feel but we go way back and you don't got shit to worry about. I just wanted to holla at you", she continued. "Loyalty word is that you're the woman who shot one of the lil workers in my crew and his mother", she informed me. "Like I said don't believe everything you hear", I spoke up. "Man keep it real with and stop acting like I got on a wire or against you", she snapped. "My bad but like I said I don't know who to trust". "If I was on tip, I didn't have to swindle you here Loyalty I would have just come and hollered at you but in a different manner. We go way back and you was always a loyal bitch", she said. I gave her a slight smirk. "Don't get me wrong I was pissed at first but then I hollered at a few sources and got something I may want to hear". "What's that", I asked confused. "Look at the dude you killed, how did you know him", she said? "Actually, he was brought to me saying he had some insight on some shit". "He wouldn't talk so I made the decision of his fate", I responded. "Well whatever hunch you had about the information he was holding was true", she shrugged her shoulders. "What you mean Sugah"? "I mean he knew who killed your mother because he was there". I'm pretty sure that's why he was brought to you right", she said. "Yea something like that", I said puzzled. "I wasn't able to get all the information of what he knew exactly but I'm going to find out", she told me. "You my dawg forever and I want you to get justice for your mother whether it was legal justice or street justice". "I'm not against you my baby and I can promise you that", she confirmed to me. "I hear you and appreciate it", I told her. "If you want to turn the city up, I got your back no matter what", she assured me. "Just don't shoot any more of my workers, do your research before you start pulling triggers ok", she mugged me. The look I gave her was like bitch please. "Just let me know who the issue is with and I'll handle it". "Well Loyalty let me get outta here money calls, just remember what I said. She hugged me tight. "Please take care of yourself and focus on everything", she preached to me. I respect her for coming to talk to me though. I needed to come up with the ultimate plan to start striking this muthafuckah. I decided to go sit at the trap and just watch some shit. Dollah is supposed to hit me when the drop is set.

Walking into the house with a few people there. The

dude Spooks and some other guy was there. I sat on the couch and played tired. "Wassup Ma", the guy said. "Hey," I replied all dry. The other dude came and sat next to me. "I'm Spooks", he announced himself. "I think I've met you", I mentioned. "You're the one I gave a ride to, right?", I asked? "Yea that's me", he smiled. "What are you smiling for"? "I'm just high Ma and always smiling", he explained. "So, you and Envy are messing around huh", I continued. "Shhhh", he sat up. "Look what me and her got going on is our business", he frowned. "Envy is my business", I snapped quickly. QC walked out of his office and stood there and looked at us. Him just standing there had my blood boiling. "What happen to your face Unk", I smirked. "Cut myself shaving yesterday", he told me. "What are you doing here, don't you have somewhere to be", he stared at me. "Actually, I don't so here I am", I said. "Well make yourself useful while you're here. Gone on in the back room and count the bags of money for me, he instructed. "I have a few runs to make and will be out for a while. Make sure you turn the cameras back on Tony when the man leaves". "Ok boss", he nodded. You can tell whatever was in his phone had his full attention though. "Spooks come with me. Loyalty stay here until I get back". Gathering his things, they headed out.

This dude Tony was the Levi type I swear. Like why do he even keep him around? Especially if he is stealing. This man QC a muthafuckah boy I tell you. I wouldn't be surprised if he wasn't up to some bullshit. That's maybe why he called me back here. But it would definitely come to light in due time. He got a rude awakening coming his way and didn't even know it. My thoughts were interrupted by my phone ringing. It was Dollah. "Hello", I answered. "What are you doing you good, I haven't heard from you all morning", he asked. "Yea I'm good I'm at the trap counting this money", I told him. "You sure that's a good idea you better stay calm Loyalty", he said. "I'm good but I have to play it off ya know", I assured him. This man knows he is really growing on me. I can't believe we have been kicking it like we have in the midst of all this bullshit. I just hope he is really on our side because it's going to hurt to kill his ass.

"I called because I wanted to tell you that the meeting is set up for Saturday at 5 p.m. So, you need to be loyal to you and Envy", he told me. "I couldn't come to the meeting with you guys, but I'll be close to believe that okay ". "So, who are we meeting with? I asked Dollah? you mean with this Cuban do he's supposed to have some information for you all he won't tell me what it is also he's trying to kill the beef between you and his people that QC started after your mom died. So, you want me to come to the truck and keep you company he asked nah that's okay it won't take me long plus QC left this n**** Tone here. oh yeah you better watch that n**** He is annoying and talks too much. Well after I link with Envy later, I'll call you and you're going to cook dinner right. do you want me to cook for you huh he laughs you know I got you just hit me.

Sitting here thinking of a plan to get QC and counting this money. Tone was sitting there looking all stupid. "Hand me that stack you just counted lil momma. Let me see if you are really on point with yo shit. Cause I don't get why QC got you here", he said. Well, I'm here because word it's a thief among us and I'm just trying to make sure we are good", I responded. He laughed. "Oh, yea a thief huh". I just staired at his dumb ass like niggah you know that cause you're the thief. "What's so funny?", I asked? "You lil momma, that's what's funny. You use words like "among us, and we are good", he continued. I turned my music off, stopped counting and gave him my full attention. "What's so funny about that niggah", I snapped. "Girl you are not a part of shit don't nobody knows who you are lil girl. You just showed up and all this bullshit going on. I mean we know your Lady J daughter and all. I just don't remember you being here rebuilding shit after your mother left. This QC shit now and you better watch yourself bitch", he smirked. Leaning back in his chair like he did something.

Before you knew I had his ass flipped over in that damn chair with my gun in his mouth. "What's Lady J's is most definitely mine muthafukah. You got some muthafuking nerve talking to me like that. "Lil momma chill", he pleaded. Hands in the air and face full of fear. "As of this being QC shit, that's what I find funny. "I was just joking", he said. "You were right though I wasn't here, cause if I was, I'd have been killed yo ass", I mugged him. I could feel myself slipping into a dark place and all I could see was red. I cocked my gun putting one in the head. "Please, please, don't", he begged. Soon as I was about to bust his thieving, talking to much ass in the head the door flew open. "Hey, Sis, what the fuck", Envy spoke. It was her and QC. "STOP Loyalty", QC yelled. I let Tone shirt go and shot next to him inches away from his head. Envy grabbed my gun and pulled me toward the door. "Get up Tone", QC instructed. He stood up and we noticed his ass pissed on himself. "Damn Tone, who's the bitch now pissy ass", I laughed. "What the fuk is going on in here", QC asked? "Ya man's talk too much and better learn to respect me or I'll kill his snake ass myself", I told him. "What the fuck did you say Tone", QC yelled. "I, I, I, just told her this your shit now and she better get on board", he stuttered. "Naw what happened to all that bitch shit you was saying. All that Lady J shit and what not", I mugged him. "Bitch like I said this QC shit now and you better get on board yo momma gone. We don't know you and don't fucking plan too, stupid ass lil girl. QC you a fool to think she is a asset", he ranted. "Tone, you got some fucking nerve bumpin your lips like this" QC turned to him. "Boss with all respect Envy causes enough problems now you bring this lil bitch back here to be in charge too", he looked at us. "Don't start with me Tone", Envy turned around. "I'm not scared of you Envy them other niggahs may be but bitch you can't count your days too", he laughed. "QC yo old ass so busy running around plotting shit but you

It's On Now | 115

are blinded by the pussy you blind on what's really coming". Envy and I made eye contact confused. QC grabbed Tone and slammed him up against the wall. "Niggah what the fuck you talking about", he yelled. "Everybody know you fucking Envy and all y'all days are numbered. Lady J's legacy will die once and for all just like her dirty ass", he smirked. "Fuck a snake serpent is coming for all y'all ass", he pushed QC off him. My sister walked out with tears in her eyes. I mean I was stuck like damn who the fuck is serpent. Next thing you know Envy came back in shot that niggah in both his legs. Walking over, standing over him pointing her gun at him. "Bitch I've been wanting to kill your ass a long time ago but QC spared you. But now since I see the greed coming out of you, God couldn't stop the wrath I'm going to place on your whole family. Know this though I'm personally going to wipe your fucking lifeline off this bitch. Taking me as a joke, disrespecting my sister, as well mentioning my mother like this.

I grabbed my gun and pointed it at him as well. "We are both going to kill everything you love or everyone that loved you. I bet a bitch be scared to even say rest in peace yo thirsty Levi ass", I told him. "Girls let me handle this and y'all will get y'all chance. Take a walk", QC said. He stood over him blocking us from shooting him. "Move QC", Envy said. He pushed her hand, lowering her gun. "I said I got this", he repeated. She looked over at me. I raised my gun to QC. "You fucking my little sister", I was pissed. Even though I knew already here was my chance to just kill his ass. He just looked at me without breaking eye contact. "Loyalty, I said I got this", he said. "I said are you fuking my little sister and I'm not going to ask you again". "YES, and have", Tone yelled! He then placed his foot on Tone's leg. Tone yelled. My gun was still pointed at QC. "ANSWER ME," I yelled. I looked at my sister with so much fire in my eyes. "Envy you fucking QC", I asked her. She looked at me and put her head down. "Yes", she answered. "Don't shoot Envy, I'm pregnant", she blurted out. As she was talking Spooks walk in. "Pregnant", he repeated. "Yea yo bitch fuckin QC", he yelled. "You fuking QC Envy", he asked? She looked at him and put her head down. He looked at QC with such envy in his eyes. It was that moment I knew I could get Spooks against QC now. "EVERYBODY the fuck out, I got this shit right here", QC yelled. "Loyalty put that fucking gun down before you make the wrong move. Spooks get out your feelings wrap his ass up and take this hoe ass niggah to the basement. Envy it's time for you and your sister to leave", he said.

QC plays everything so smooth and calm at all times. Especially when he was super pissed. He knew he fucked up and I bet his mind was racing hard. A well as whatever plan he was cooking up had been ruined. He then walked out past us all. Envy and I followed behind him. She reached out to grab Spooks' arm. He snatched away. "Who baby is that?", he asked her? "Baby I don't know", she dropped a tear. He looked up at her and smiled. "Don't baby me Envy, I'm done with your ass. I want a blood test until then stay the fuk away from me", he snapped at her. "Spooks", she said. He slammed the door to the room in her face. She just stood there for a second. I could tell him finding out about her and QC hurt more than me finding out. "You ok sis", I asked? She looked at me with those hazel eyes and shook her head no. "Wait for me in the car please", I told her. She walked right past the room QC was in. He kept calling out to her. I stood in the doorway just muggin 'him. "QC I can't believe you; I know my mother is turning in her grave behind this". "Loyalty not now", he responded. "Yea you handle Tone but we are definitely going to talk. You dirty muthafukah you", I said. "Girl get the fuck out of here, I said not right now", he told me. Slamming his head into the pile of coke on his desk. That shit shocked me because I had never seen this side of him. I mean him yelling and shit but this nothing to say shit was weird. Envy and I needed to make a move and make it this weekend. I shut his door and walked off. I can't wait to kill this muthafuckah dawg, I thought to myself. Heading to the car, Envy and I were about to go talk about all this shit. Plus, I needed to get in touch with Spooks. I want to know what QC does to Tone. One this QC hated was a snitch and he did a lot of talking. Plus, the QC I know was think just like I was. Who the fuck is this serpent he talking about?

12.

Tie His Ass Up Spooks

"Look Spooks I want you to clean that fool up and take him to the basement. Tie his hoe ass up and I'll be down there", I said. Spooks was pissed but his ass better get out his feelings. "I know you are mad and all but don't let pussy distract you. Get his ass down there NOW", I told him. If your ass want to live and continue to make money this way you better do what the fuck I said", I continued. "Alright boss", he smirked. I yelled for lil dawg on the porch to help him carry him down there. "Damn Tone what happened to you", he asked? "This what the fuck gone happen to you if you ever cross me", I scolded him. "You don't have to worry about me boss, I am nothing like that", he responded. "Trap closed for the rest of the day. I don't want NOBODY here today", I instructed. I went into my office and slammed my door. Sitting at my desk pissed off to the max. Pulling my bottle of Duse' out and hitting my blow. This fool really just did that hoe shit. He knew what I was trying to do, now Spooks is acting all weird. Might have to pop his ass cause I'll be damned if he crosses me next. Or if he thinks he is getting Envy she's mine. I hit another line after a sip from the bottle. Pregnant though damn I might have to kill her and a baby if she don't get rid of that bitch Loyalty. I was still going through with my plan fuck it. I know one thing though I'm about to go whoop the shit out of Tone all night. Then make Spooks take his ass out to the spot. Bury that bitch alive since he got so much to say.

When I walked into the basement Spooks had his ass tied to the chain sitting in the middle of the room. I took off my Moncler and rolled up my sleeves. Punching his ass so hard in the jaw. "I told you that your mouth was going to get you killed", I smirked. "C'mon man you really want to do this", he pleaded. I punched his ass again. About fifteen minutes later my phone rang. It was the play I had been waiting on. Tone was fucked up but hanging in there. "Watch him", I told Spooks. I headed upstairs whipping the blood off my hands with the towel I had.

I was maybe gone an hour before I returned. When I got back into the basement they were gone. The basement had been cleaned up and shit. Thinking to myself knowing Spooks he bout done just killed the niggah, fucking up my fun. Least he cleaned up the mess though. I decided to go home and get cleaned up. I need to figure some shit out.

Driving out to the spot thinking so hard. What the fuck is really going on though. Tone laid in the backseat crying for his life. "Look, Spooks man just let me go bro", he pleaded. "You know I can't do that. "Tone that mouth of yours done got you into some deep shit", I told him.

I pulled up to this spot we had in the woods. The final resting spot for the loudmouth ass niggah. Turning the lights off as I pulled down the dirt road. "Look Spooks before you kill me you tell that bitch Loyalty, I'll see her in hell, right next to her mother" he laughed. Reaching in his pocket grabbing some paper with a number on it. "Tell Envy to call this number and she'll be surprised at what they know. I grabbed the paper and put it in the glovebox.

I then pulled his ass out the car and put him in the ditch that was ready for him. "Man don't do this dawg I'll leave and never return", he begged. "That's not my choice to make plus the money I'm getting behind this is worth it". "QC is going down and I know this. I can save you Spooks. I've been under cover building a case on him from back in the day", he said. "Niggah what you just say", I frowned. Before I knew I dropped his ass in that ditch and put two in his head. Setting the body on fire before fleeing. Running to the car and pulling off so fast. As bad as I didn't want to, I called Envy and told her to meet me at her house now. She agreed, so we headed straight there after changing cars.

13.

Y'all Need To know (Envy)

My mind was racing as I headed to my house to meet Spooks. I knew he was pissed at me behind Tone talking about QC. I texted my sister and told her to pull up as well. Since I was supposed to meet her at momma's house. So many questions ran through my head cuz Tone does talk a lot but some of his shit is creditable. QC had to go and I know how envious he could be. I don't want him to hurt Spooks behind me. Spooks is a solid dude and I love him. It's just a deep connection between me and QC though. Behind closed doors he's definitely a different vibe. As I'm riding, the next song on my playlist was the Mozzy song Unfortunately. The words really hit home with me. What could possibly happen next, I thought.

Pulling up the same time Loyalty did, Spooks was already parked in the back. They both got out of their cars and followed me in. We all sat around my kitchen table. He didn't say anything to me at first, he just stared at me. Like if looks could kill I'd be dead as hell. I broke the silence after lighting my cigarette. "So, what did you need to say", I asked him. He mugged me. "Put that cigarette out since you are pregnant and it may be mine", he said. "Cut all that Spooks get to the point you told me don't say shit to you about it until you get a test. So don't get to barking orders over here", I snapped back. Loyalty just looked at us as she sat back in her chair. "Look I'm not in the mood to play with Envy for real", he turned to me. "Spook you can let all the hostility out of your chest later why are we here", I interrupted him. "Envy just tell me how you can be so honest with me, beat up bitches that was on me. Sleep with me, tell me you love me and shit but the whole time you fucking QC", he continued. I was stuck for a while; I mean at a complete loss for words. Because the look my sister had on her face was of a broken heart about that. "Spooks I'm sorry, ok one thing led to another and I'm sorry. I do love you but I fucked up", I told him. "Envy you don't love nobody but the streets and your heart is cold as ice. You wouldn't be in the situation if you would have kept it real. QC don't give a fuck about you", he shook his head.

"Look let me get to the facts iight", he sat back. I just felt so bad I couldn't even look at him because he was right. I was so deep in the streets my heart was ice cold. No matter how much I wanted to love, I couldn't let the streets go. "So, for one that fool QC I got it in for both of y'all. He is trying to shut y'all out of what your mother has built. That's all he talks about. He couldn't do it how it was planned with just one of you away. That fool is very intimidated by you Loyalty", he explained. "So is that what Tone told you ", Loyalty asked with a puzzled look on her face. "I know personally that QC was jealous of your mother because he was deeply in love with her. That's all he talks about especially when he is all coked up and drunk". "What", she asked. "Yea one day he said that y'all should have been his kids, but she wanted to fuck the Cuban dude so bad. So, he had to get them both out of the way. He never really said he had her killed or had anything to do with it but I know he did something", Spooks explained to us. What I was wondering in my head had my blood boiling. So, this fool had the audacity to sleep with me and secretly wanted to be my father. Spooks interrupted my thoughts. "Tone gave me this number and said you must call them ASAP. They got the information you want. He even told me that he has been working undercover building a case on QC. So, you might want to chill out from the trap", he said. He then got up and proceeded to leave. I followed him to the door trying to talk to him. He ignored me but before he walked out, he turned to me and said, "Envy I loved you and all I wanted in return was loyalty", closing the door behind him.

I just stood there speechless. I mean I never wanted to hurt Spooks, I love him a lot. As I watched him pull out the driveway, I texted his phone. "*I don't want no one else but you and I'm sorry baby I fucked up. Just hear me out please. I choose you Spooks*". I can tell he read it but he never responded. I plopped down on the couch and prepared for Loyalty shit next. She walked in and sat next to me. "Come here", she reached her hands. My sister hugged me so tight that I just broke down in her arms. I haven't cried like this in a very long time. I was hurt, angry, sad, and full of revenge. One thing you don't do is play around with Envy. QC ass was mine; I don't give a fuck if he is my child's father. I'm going to kill him myself. "Envy, talk to me, you don't have to deal with this alone. I got you forever lil sis", Loyalty told me. I took a deep breath and sat back on the couch.

"It all started after you went to college. I mean before you left, he would say little slick shit to me but I mean look at me who wouldn't. I want to say it was a night after one of his parties. He had rented an Airbnb and threw the biggest stripper party. I was already dating Spooks on the low back then. Spooks is the one I allowed to take my virginity back in the day. Well Spooks went out of town on business that QC sent him at the last minute. So, after the party was over, I stayed at the Airbnb. I was lit as hell so driving was out of the question. Even though I was lit I knew what was going on around me. So, after everyone had left, I started picking up a little bit. QC was laying on the couch fucked up. "Did he take advantage of you Envy", she cut me off. "Calm down sis, listen to me like you said", I told her. "I mean looking back after tonight yes, he did. Anyways after cleaning up a lil bit, I went and took a shower. Once I was done, I went and sat on the couch across from QC. I started rolling up and flicking through the channels and texting Spooks. Nobody knew about me and Spooks but Dolla. QC sat up on the couch and looked at me without saying a word. I don't know what was going through his head but the lust was in his eyes. "Envy can I tell you something", I recalled him saying. HE told me how much he admired my street capability and how hard I went for the paper. He said that he had been watching me in a way he didn't think he should have. I was puzzled at first but kept listening. I don't know if it was the liquor or the E pill, I popped at the party but QC was looking good as hell. I mean his old man was looking real daddish I smirked. I told him I appreciate his honesty but maybe he should go to bed. We talked and talked for hours. The stuff he expressed to me had my mind blown, and I was turned on. He walked over to me and grabbed me, picking me, and carrying me to the kitchen. Don't get me wrong I had so many thoughts running through my head. I just couldn't stop the moment that was happening between us. After that night it was on from there. I mean we both agreed we should keep it between us and then he started becoming possessive. Like getting upset when he would see Spooks and I together. I remember one time he ordered a hit on a guy I started seeing. It caught me by surprise that he did that shit. His excuse was that dude told him he was going to rob me blind one night. But now after all this I see that it was a lie. Dude wasn't even the hood type.

"Well little sis I'm not mad at you or blame you", Loyalty said. "He knows he was wrong and if momma was here, he would have been dead. "I'm not going to come down hard on you this time but you have to start thinking Envy. I don't want you putting yourself in positions to be hurt. When you are hurting so am I", she continued. I couldn't say anything because she was right. I have to make better decisions and time to raise hell though. I had to get even by any means necessary. I also needed to figure out if I wanted this baby. "Loyalty, I don't know if I want to keep this baby", I said. "What do you mean sis you don't know", she asked? "Well, I live the fast life and not only do I live it I love it, Loyalty. I don't want to put my child in that type of environment. Look where that led us sis we are in too deep. Our line of work in the family business just won't sit right with a child around", I explained. "Envy we don't have to live this life baby sis we don't. Momma left us enough money to thrive thru life. You can change Envy just try", she responded. "Loyalty, you're not listening. I love the fast life and I refuse to stop. I'll always be a street runner. With the father being Spooks or QC, the street life will be in my child", I said. We both sat there in silence for about five minutes.

"We are going to get his ass and everyone rolling with him at this point is guilty", Loyalty said. "Look, who is this number he gave you", she asked? "I don't know sis but we ought to find out", I responded. I called the number and couldn't recognize the voice. "This Envy and I was told you had info for me and my sister that we needed to know ". "Meet me at Bufford park in the back alley off of Union street in an hour", the voice said. They hung up. I don't know if we should go but I knew my sister didn't want to hear that. "Come on sis let's go see what this is all about", I told her.

I went in the basement to my lil room I had set up for us to be war ready. I gave Loyalty two 357's and I grabbed my nine and the pump. I texted Spooks and told him where we were going. Loyalty told Dollah as well but we informed them if they didn't hear from us to come show out. We hopped into my sister's car and headed out. I rolled me up a blunt and loaded my gun as she drove. She circled the block a few times to make sure that no one was trying to ambush us. Loyalty backing in the alley all the way back. That way we could see if anyone pulled in or came up from the dark. We sat there and waited. "Envy you ok", she asked? "Yea just ready to find out what's going on and who is behind this", I answered. "No, I mean you sure you want to do this we can leave. I don't want to put the baby at risk sis", she grabbed my hand. "Sis, I put the baby at risk when I got pregnant", I said, cooking my gun.

About twenty minutes later we could see a shadow walking towards us from down by the basketball court. It was so dark though you couldn't see their faces. I leaned my seat back with the pump ready to blow. As they got closer, we noticed it was a light skinned man. He walked in the front of the car and just stood there. Loyalty flashed the lights twice and he just stood there. "Stay here", she told me. Loyalty hopped out the gun in hand.

That girl really don't give a fuck about shit when she in protection mode. She walked up to the man and stood there.

When I got out the car and walked over to the man standing in front of my car, he never said one word. "Who are you and what do you want with us", I asked? He didn't say anything at first and began to reach into his pocket. I pointed my gun at "don't you do it". "Wait it's just my phone, don't shoot" he held a hand up. Proceeding to scuffle in his pocket Envy jumped and pointed her gun. He had an accent when he spoke. "I'm Joel Rodriguez I'm y'all father and I came to warn you", he said. My mouth dropped and I turned to Envy. "What did he say?", she asked me? "He said he is our father Envy", I said. "I came to warn y'all about someone in your circle", he told me. Envy walked up to him and punched him in his face so hard. "You mean to tell me you are not dead and you never came for us", she yelled. I put my gun in the back of my pants and grabbed her. "Chill sis even though you're not wrong", I tried to calm her down. "You better talk quick, she not easy to hold back", I warned him. "Look I deserve that", he held his jam. "You got a mean punch baby girl, just like your mother", he laughed.

The next thing you know we were ambushed. Bullets began flying left and right. I mean someone really was shooting at us. It was so dark we couldn't see anything but us from up here. I pulled my gun and started shooting back into the dark towards the court. If I don't shoot shit, it will at least back they ass up. "Get back sis, get in the car", I yelled! Joel caught one to the arm as he shot back the opposite way of me. "Fuk", he yelled! I pulled him back towards our car, Envy hopped in the driver's seat. I shot a few more times to make sure they weren't bold enough to walk up here. Once we were in the car my sister pulled out of there.

Flying down Dickinson towards Madison. A black Malibu started following us. "Get to the highway I got a spot. Head towards 68th street", he instructed. "Well, I gotta lose this car behind me. Whoever got some major balls" she yelled. She flew up Madison towards Burton highway, zig zagging through side streets. "I want you to hit the darkest street you can sis and stop. If they hit us, they hit us but I'm about to flip that bitch", I told her. She hit a few more zig zags and stopped full force. I then jumped out and lit that bitch up. He was on point because he didn't stop. But he never expected that from me though. He shot back once and hit the back window. I just kept blasting. "BAM, BAM, BAM, BAM "! "BAM, BAM"! I heard someone yell "Fuk he hit". Jumping back into the car as the passenger car door opened. "Pull off sis go", I yelled! She merked off as fast as she could. A car parked on the street pulled off behind us. "Somebody else is following us, " she yelled. "Bust a right on College, take them down the street by the Elks ", I told her. She did just that. "Can you shoot", I asked him? "Like never before we shake this car and I got a spot", he responded. Envy rolled down the back windows as she slowed down to stop. I told him to shoot out the window. I jumped out as soon as she stopped and started blasting. Lighting that muthafukah up bet they didn't expect that coming. Right idea but the wrong bitches. I hopped back into the car and she pulled off. Flying down the hall towards the highway. He gave us directions to an address.

Once we were there the garage door began to open. "Pull in here", he instructed. Some lady came running out straight to his side of the car. She was so beautiful. Long curly hair pulled into a ponytail, no makeup, and a long Gucci robe. "Oh my gosh honey, are you ok", she cried. "Yes, just a lil wound, it went straight through", he said, getting out. "Go get the kit baby we are right behind you", he instructed her. "Y'all come with me", he summoned. I looked at Envy and she nodded in agreement. We followed behind him into the big ass house. I mean it was huge as hell. He led us into a room not far from the garage.

The room was nicely decorated too. It had black carpet all through it with red couches. As we looked around, I noticed the back wall was filled with pictures. It was pictures of my sister and I growing up. He even had pictures of me on my school campus. "This shit creepy as hell Loyalty", Envy said, walking up to the wall. Our mothers picture was in the middle of the wall. Either he was obsessed, the man who killed her, or he really was our father. "Have a seat girls ", he insisted. We both sat down on the couch next to each other and right across from them. "Do you y'all smoke?", he asked light a phat ass blunt. "I do", Envy spoke up. "Knowing your condition, you shouldn't but after what just happened, I'll give you a pass", he told her. She looked at me quickly. "What condition are you talking about", she asked? "I know that you are pregnant so you shouldn't be smoking", he smirked. "You know an awful damn lot so you need to start talking", she said. At this point I agree on that, because how does he know that she is pregnant?

I decided to speak up because I can see the anger in Envy eyes forming. "So, who are you and why do you have pictures of us", I asked? "Can you give us a moment to speak in private", he told the lady cleaning his arm. He waited till she was gone and got up to shut the door. After he shut the door, he walked over to the bar and pressed a button. The back of the bar where the liquor turned. It turned into a room. "Come on we'll talk in here", he waved. We walked behind him. In the room was a wall full of monitors. Showing every angle and inch of this house. It was a pool table and a flat screen mounted on the wall, with one long couch. Envy and I sat together on the sofa. He sat on the pool table staring at us. "Look Batman who the hell are you", Envy broke the silence. "Watch your mouth when speaking to me young lady", he told her. "Naw you watch your mouth when talking to her ", I interrupted. "Look I don't want to argue with you girls ok", he threw his hands up. "I am Joel Rodriguez. Your mother called me JR. I'm your father. I have those pictures of y'all because until your mother died, she sent them to me. After she passed, I kept a close eye on you both. I was so furious now that he said that I had so many questions. "I don't believe you", Envy said. He put his head down as he reached into his pocket for his wallet. "Your mother's real name is JaMyah Zion Wallace aka Lady J", he smirked. "Did you think your last name was just randomly picked. He did make since there, I thought. "Look I'm sorry I never popped up sooner", he told us. "Well why you pop up now we don't got shit for you, and we die before you think you're getting anything out of my mommas", Envy spoke up. "I don't want anything from your mothers Envy, my paper tail is long", he responded. "So, what is it that you want then", I said. "I just want to give y'all some information I know as well as try to get to know y'all", he explained. "What information you got", Envy said. She was not letting up, I bet if I wasn't here, she would shoot his ass. Even though it took so long I'm still glad to see momma didn't kill him like I thought. "Envy chill let's just hear him out, he may know something that can help us. "I'm just saying why help us now we've been needing you", she went on. He just sat there smoking his cigarette. "Are you done bitching, just like your momma", he smirked. She rolled her eyes, folded her arms, and sat back on the couch. "I've always kept a close eye on both of y'all. I'm stepping in now because why would I stand back and let you be a target", he stared at her. "Just tell us", I butted in. "Well to cut to the chase how the fuck QC be a possibility of being your child's father", he asked her? She looked at me shocked that he knew that. "Don't look at me I didn't tell him", I threw my hands up. "Like I keep saying I've been keeping a close eye on you both", he said. "I will holla at QC though cause he had to know I would come for him behind this", he went on. "What you mean behind this", I asked? "I mean he knew damn well he shouldn't have laid a finger on my daughter in that way. He knows I've never liked him ever. Your mother knew I wanted to kill him and she protected him. The day I left I got into it with your mom real bad. She had found out I shot him at the gambling house. After I told her I would leave him alone. I came home and she flipped out fighting me. I got so mad she was defending him and her hitting me I slapped her. She chased me with her gun blazing behind me. I was so damn scared she grazed me too", he told us. He lifted up his shirt and showed us the scar on his side. I remember him being chased but I don't remember why, I was so young. "Why did you shoot him? "Envy asked? "Well, he was hating on me and your mom's relationship. He wanted her to himself. I found out that they fucked and he was the seducer. So, when I saw him, I tried to kill him. QC knew I wasn't for no games and he still tried me. Even though she said it was an accident and it meant nothing, I wanted blood". "Why didn't you come back", I asked? "Your mother wasn't having it. After a few attempts of trying, she told me she would kill me if I showed up again. Knowing your mother, she was serious, I fucked up when I hit her and I knew she really wanted blood. When I heard she was killed I lost it and have been looking into it all these years. I finally found out why she was killed and by who. Then I heard he was after " y'all and QC ", he explained to us. "Who", we both asked? "Y'all man Dollah not right", he looked dead in my eyes.

When I say so much rage grew in my heart. My body was on fire. You would have thought my body was a gun and I had been loaded with fire bullets. "Man, Dollah ain't did shit, how we know you ain't just trying to start some shit", Envy chuckled. I just sat in a trance because I gave all of myself to the man, I've been looking for all my life. "Envy I have no reason to lie and I got proof", he emphasized. Standing and walking to the desk in the corner. Grabbing a big brown folder. He definitely had both of our full attention. As I tuned in, I could not notice how much we looked like him. Momma's ways and attitude but daddies look. I mean we damn near triplets. Pulling out a picture of a couple. I recognized that the guy momma had cut his tongue out. Telling us that they were once rolling with him and momma getting hella money. The couple started using the supply running off and fucking up money. "One time I was so mad they were short with some pape on a big deal. So, we ended up taking their son for a couple weeks. They loved him because they found the money really quick. So, we gave them one last chance, because we were close to them. Then after some time he ran off with some drugs. Your mom saw him talking to a detective and she cut his tongue out", he said.

That took me back instantly. I knew for sure it made Envy think back. She was so fascinated with that moment. Plus, we both were there to see it done. I will never forget that crazy shit. Our mother was so damn ruthless when it came down to certain shit. Envy interrupted the story and my thoughts. "So, you mean to tell me that Dolla is the little boy, and that was his dad", she asked. "Yes, that's exactly what I'm telling you", he answered. "Dollah has an uncle named Know It All and he has been helping him with this plan from my understanding". "I met Know It All but Dolla said he was his grandfather. He told me many stories about mom and some about you as well", I mentioned.

Envy sat there quietly for a minute just taking it all in. "So, you mean to tell me that Dollah killed our mother", I asked. "What I'm saying is he was informed by someone very close to me to take y'all out", he said. "What do you mean hired?", Envy sat up. "Yea I know everything and we will all end this together", he stood up. "Who the fuck killed our mother", she continued? "It was my ex-wife Rosa'. The woman I was married to back in Cuba. After I met your mother, I completely left Rosa' alone. NO phone calls, visits, or communication. I cut Rosa' dry from the product and all. Well, this crazy bitch found out the reason why and wanted revenge. "So, you're the reason why our mother is dead", my sister yelled. "No, I QC is the reason your mother is dead. He is the one who informed her of what me and your mother had going on. He told her about me and your mothers plan about taking you two and leaving the game. QC ruined my life because he wanted your mother in a way, he couldn't have her. He chose greed over loyalty. This mothafukah had the audacity to take Dollah in after we killed his parents. Then he disappeared for a long time and came back as a teenager back to QC. QC had sent him to be raised by Rosa'. See Rosa' was a very well-known trained killer. She is the one who pulled the trigger. I need yall to help me find the bitch and kill her ass. Not only was yall life ruined but so was mine", he began to cry. I could see the hurt in his eyes when he spoke about my mother. "So where is this bitch at, Envy asked. "We have to find her, she has been in hiding ever since", he told us. Soon as he was about to say something else his phone rang. He stopped mid-sentence and answered. "Look girls stay here make yourself comfortable. I'll be back in a second. I have a meeting out back and will try not to be long. No matter what, don't come out there you hear me" he said.

After he walked out Envy burst out in tears. I couldn't do anything but hold her and cry too. This shit is crazy as hell. After all these years our father has never been far away. His wife killed our mother. QC and Dolla working with his crazy bitch. My mother died of greed and bitterness. "Loyalty, what do we do?", she sobbed. "Sis don't break down on me now, we gotta handle this shit". "Baby sis I got you no matter what and whether we are ready to accept it daddy is here now", I hugged her. "I can't believe Dollah was really bold from the jump", she said. "I'm still shocked by that", I told her.

In my mind I was furious and hurt. I couldn't dare let her see my weakness right now. One thing I do know is my heart was just shattered. Like I would have rather he just shoot me in cold blood then to play with my heart and intelligence. Like damn niggah I know you want revenge but damn you a cold muthafuckah. I'm going to kill him myself and all by myself. He will be the first to go watch how I play his ass. Right idea, wrong bitch. I don't give a damn if momma did kill your whole family. Its rules and levels to this shit. "Loyalty, what are we going to do sis?", she asked me. "We are going to make everybody pay. "We are going to come full force and get it back in blood", I assured her. It was definitely time to turn it up a notch.

Our dad walked back in and sat between us. "Look girls I know this is a lot to take in. I don't expect y'all to just accept me into y'all lives. But I do want to help y'all get closure", he sobbed. Envy stared at him for a few seconds and just broke down in his arms. Watching them hugging and crying together made me cry so hard. My sister needed him way more than me. To watch all the hurt and pain leave her body and transform onto his back was magical. I mean it gave me the peace knowing I wasn't the only one to love her unconditionally. He hugged us so tight and just cried. We all cried together; all we were missing was our mother.

He had the woman there fix us something to eat and prepare a room for us. We decided to stay the night with him. Envy was very quiet. I knew she was very upset and war ready. She's always so loud so when she's quiet you better worry. I just hope she doesn't stress herself too badly. Spooks isn't responding to her messages or text at all. I could tell she really loved him and was so hurt. Meanwhile she kept declining QC calls. I really can't believe he would even look at her like that. I mean even knowing what you and my mother did. Why even use her like that. Then have the audacity to be a possibility to her child. I know she was going crazy inside.

Once we ate and settled down Envy went to sleep. My dad was sitting up in his office counting money, and cleaning guns. I stood in the doorway watching him. He hadn't looked up so he didn't notice me at first. Well at least I thought so. As I was walking away, he called my name and said something to me I haven't heard since I was a kid. When I was little, he would always say "Loyalty my royalty, the one I'll love for eternity". Hearing that gave my body chills. I mean I never forgot it. That was icing on the cake for me, he was our father. Tears began to just fall down my face. I was happy as hell to see he was alive but so very mad that it took this for him to show himself. Like thanks for coming clutch for us but damn we've needed you dude. He looked up at me just watching me cry. I wiped my face and stared back. "Loyalty, come sit down, " he insisted. I walked over and sat across from him at his desk. "Help me clean these, he threw me a towel. I looked at the guns he had spread out on his desk. "Look baby girl I want to apologize for not trying harder to be your life. I allowed your mothers anger and my stubbornness to keep me away. I was so caught up in the streets and all three of you needed me. I'll never forgive myself for that. You and your sister mean the world to me, I will spend my last days on Earth trying to make it up.

14.

The Plot Thickens

After staying up late counting money with my dad, I was tired. I decided to lay low today. No calls or text I needed to clear my mind. Plus, I'm still upset as hell that someone shot at us like that. I mean tried to chase us down. That didn't stop the anger I felt for Dollah. Like I understand the reason behind your revenge. He is definitely going about in a pussy way. I would have rather you just killed me. Instead, you want to challenge me.

I needed to think of something quick. Then it hit me we gotta get QC first. Since Rosa' still out here Dolla will lead us to her. Especially if she is the one behind this shit. Momma said cut your grass and the snake will come to you. It was time to turn it up a notch. I called my homegirl CoCo. I'm definitely going to need her and her squad. She agreed to meet me tomorrow at East Kentwood track at about noon.

Sitting on this deck mind racing. I was ready to fuck this city up by myself. At this point anybody can die the way I'm feeling. Envy came walking out and sat next to me. "Wassup baby sis", I acknowledged her. "Hey, Loyalty, I decided not to keep the baby", she spoke out. "What?",

I sat up in shock. "Yes, you heard me right sis", she said. "Why though Envy ", I asked? "It's too much going on right now", she sighed. "Envy I got you no matter what you will not have to raise the baby alone", I told her. "Loyalty, I really messed up with Spooks and I don't want QC to be the father", she started to cry. Seeing her hurt made me want to kill his ass even more. I was too young to protect my mother but I was damn sure going to war behind my sister. I told Envy we have to get QC first, to get all the information we can from him. Then we get Dollah in which he will lead us to Rosa'. Once we get her then we get revenge for our mother", I explained. She agreed with me and told me she needed to make a few phone calls. I decided to go shower and get dressed.

I called up QC and just like I thought he answered on the first ring. Especially since has been calling nonstop since the shooting. I told him about the shooting and he didn't seem shocked at all. Honestly, he gave me vibes that he was behind the shit. I played it cool though, even though my blood was boiling. I told him we were waiting for word of who the lil dudes was. I also asked him if he had heard anything. Two shootouts like that somebody knows something. This Grand Rapids somebody knows something. Of course, he lied dirty muthafuckah. He asked where I was and I told him Loyalty had us hiding out in a room in Muskegon. I asked him to meet at my mom's place so we could talk. I can sneak away later. We have to come get clothes. He was hesitant but agreed after I mentioned the baby. I told him I decided to leave the game and was taking the baby. Mentioning my mother's safety got his attention as well. When I said that he was really down to go. Remembering him asking me about it a few times.

My sister was in the shower I grabbed the keys to make a run. Sneaking off to see Spooks. Enough is enough, he was going to talk to me. As I crept down his street, I noticed three cars in his driveway. One was his, one was unfamiliar, and the last looked just like the one that shot at us. It had bullet holes through it too. I went and parked down the street. Walking through the alley in the back. I still had a key to the back door. Creeping in through the backdoor and stepping into the kitchen. They didn't notice shit either and told his ass he needed cameras out here. The mirror in the kitchen reflected the living room clearly too. So, I could see a woman sitting on his lap and two dudes standing there. I just listened for a minute. "What the fuck happened", Spooks spoke. "We did what the fuck you asked and got clapped the fuck up", one dude said. "Where is Envy ", he asked them. "Man, we don't fucking know I backed off too many bullets flying", the other dude said. Now I was furious because I know damn well, he didn't do what I think. My hands started shaking and sweating. I'm about to kill them all. I took a deep breath and kept listening. "That bitch Envy be doing too much I don't fucking like her. One day I'ma beat her ass just on the strength", the bitch spoke.

When she said that I cocked the gun in my left hand and grabbed the one off my waist with the right. You would have thought they had seen a ghost when I busted in the living room. The dude standing tried to reach and grabbed his gun. Just moving a little too slow I hit his ass dead in the face with my gun, breaking his nose. Baby girl was trying to hide behind Spooks. The other dude didn't say shit he just sat down. I mean what would you do with a crazy bitch like me standing there with two loaded guns. "Honey I'm home you were looking for me", I laughed. "Envy what the fuck you doing, how did you get in here", Spooks said? "I still got my fucking key that's how. I came to talk to you but now it seems like yall got some answers I need", I mugged him. Nobody said shit and me and Spooks eyes were locked in. He knew I would shoot this bitch up no second guessing. "Plus, you so mad at me but fucking this bird", I pointed the gun at her. "Who the fuck you calling a bird", she said? "Bitch you might want to shut the fuck up before I get a game of duck hunt going on and pop you dumb ass", I told her. "Hell, you lucky I'm pregnant otherwise I'd put these guns down and give you that ass whooping you begging for", I continued. "Pregnant, this whole time I thought yo punk ass was gay", she smirked. This bitch really had me fucked up. "You got jokes huh, let's see how funny you are after this", I smirked back. I walked over and smacked that bitch so hard with my gun. Blood splattered quick too. "What the fuck Envy that's a five-thousand-dollar couch", Spooks yelled. "Boy fuck you and that ugly ass couch hell I bought it". "You're not laughing now huh bitch", I giggled. "Envy really", Spook stood up. "Shut the fuk up cause just seeing on her lap right now the way I'm feeling could get yo popped too", I snapped back. "Just calm down and say what you need to say. You shoot us all who going to give you the answer you claim you're looking for muthafuckah damn Envy chill", Spooks pleaded. "Why is that car in your driveway shot up like that", I asked? "Because your dumb ass shot at us", one of the dudes said. "Oh really", I smirked. Before I could even pull the trigger Spooks jumped in front of him. "STOP ENVY CHILL", he yelled. "So, you mean to tell me that you're killing us too", I said, dropping a tear. "Hell, naw I would not try and kill you no matter how mad I am at you", he sighed. "Spooks don't try to sweet talk me. I got a bullet for every head in this room", I told him. "Envy chill out baby. You texted me right so I sent them to look after you, that's it. They just told me you started clapping at them", he explained. "Well, what do you think when two cars following you shooting", I said. "So, calm your ass down please bae" he started walking towards me. Even though it felt so good to hear him call me bae. He always says it so sincerely with his head slightly cocked. I just couldn't trust it though.

The last conversation I had with my mom she told me that being vulnerable will reveal your weakest asset. Lock in eye to eye like a Pitbull and don't break contact. Soon as you do then you're finished. I snapped back to what was going on. "Get back Spooks seriously", I pointed my gun. "Really Envy? I just told you I sent them to protect you, not kill you or to be killed. You are paranoid as hell baby", he said. "Ok then Spook why didn't they shoot the car up in front of them that was chasing me shooting. Why did they pull up next to the car and then they turned off? These niggahs kept following us until we stopped", I spazzed. One dude put his head down shaking it. "Oh, y'all didn't tell him how your man got hit huh, well I'll tell him", I said. "They mans hopped out the backseat and shot at us twice. Then he got his ass lit the fuck up", I told him. "What", Spooks looked confused? "Yea you heard me so back that ass up or everybody dead. Yes, I love you but I'm definitely not dumb", I continued.

"Envy you really love me", he asked? "Yes, I do love you but you don't care to listen to me", I responded. "Well, you're so heartless at times how would I know, but we will get back to that in a minute", he said. He then sat back down on the couch. The look he gave me grabbing his gun vibes. He always kept his gun with a silencer on it right on the side of him. He lit a cigarette. "So is what she saying is true", he looked at the dudes. Ol girl was sitting there with a broken jaw looking dumb as hell. "Look man on some real shit QC paid us to go against what you said. Hell, we were hungry out here and you weren't paying us. We got families out here", dude said. Still holding his head down and the other holding his shirt up to his nose. "Well damn fam just like that huh. Too bad your family is going to starve now because you sided with the devil himself", Spooks mugged him. The anger in his eyes was turning me on so much. Like yes bae get their asses. He put a bullet in both their heads. Babygirl started to panic. "What you scared for you were just so tough", he turned to her. "What's your confession bitch", I walked over to her. I put the gun to her head. "You better say something", Spooks said. She started crying. "All I was told to drive here after they put a tracker on my car", she sobbed. "Who bitch", I yelled. I raised the gun as if I was going to hit her again. "Dollah", she yelled out. Spooks and I looked at each other shocked. Like damn Dollah you really want this smoke. I then shot her ass right between the eyes. "Now what", he said. "DUCK", I yelled! I saw dudes jumping out of the car. Next thing you know they were shooting this bitch up. All you heard were bullets flying, breaking shit everywhere. "Stay down, Envy", Spooks yelled. He crawled by the couch, grabbing one of his drakeos and slid me the other one. We both jumped up and began to start shooting back. Making their ass get the fuck back for sure. Spooks was shot twice. Once in the arm and the other in the hand. The one in his hand went straight through. Not soon later you could hear the tires screeching. "We gotta go to the Spooks", I cried. Seeing him bleeding was really freaking out. I love this man so much and have loved him for the last three years.

He wrapped his hand and grabbed a duffle bag and

handed it to me. "The cops will be here soon. I got this baby. Now go baby", he said. He may have it but I had to do something. I ran and got the towel wiped off the guns then put them in the hands of the two dudes. Kissed Spooks and started through the kitchen. "Wait, Envy, take this phone. I'll be fine. I will call that number as soon as I can", he told me. "I will be fine Envy", he assured me.

Once I got back to my car I sat there for a minute. I could hear the sirens approaching. I waited till I saw the ambulance pull up before I pulled off. I called Loyalty from the phone Spooks gave me, hoping she would answer. "Who is this", she answered? "This Envy I'm calling from a burner", I responded. "Spooks and I were ambushed. QC is moving in fast with no hesitation. "Are you ok", she panicked. "Yes, but Ima text you a location so we can talk about it." I said,

We were definitely going to need a distraction though. That way we can get a tracker on his car. Plus have a tail on his every move. Since he is coming like this, we gotta be ready and know he has a plan. Heading to the location where I told my sister to meet me. I had her meet me at the 76th Street Diner. She agreed so I headed there as soon as we hung up. My mind was moving a mile a minute. I hope Spooks is ok. If something happens to him it's going to be hell to pay the captain, and I'm the muthafukin captain.

As I drove all I could think of is what would my mother do right now. The only thing I could think of is her being ready to fuck the city up. I mean they really got us fucked up for real. I was so furious but I had to keep it together. I had to keep my composure through this madness this time and let my sister lead. She had to because after all this fuck the answers I just want to shoot.

It didn't take me long to arrive there. When I got there, I sat in the car for a minute, thinking of Spooks, I also thought of the baby I was carrying. Like do I really want to keep the baby after all of this? So much going on at once I swear.

Getting out of the car and heading in. She was already sitting when I walked in. She was a couple of booths back from the door. I slid into the booth across from her and just looked at her. "Hey baby sis are you ok what happened", she broke the silence. Sitting in silence for a minute because just the thought had me pissed all over again. "Well, I went to go talk to Spooks but ran up on some shit. Two of the guys that were there were the same two guys whose car we aired out last. I guess Spooks sent them to watch our back, out of respect for him. Well QC got a hold of them and paid them to shoot us up instead. We killed them and then a car full of dudes rushed the car and sprayed the house up. "Get the fuck out of here", she said shockishly. "Yes, sis QC is really trying my patience, it's time to make a move", she continued. I can say she is right because if the baby is his he showing me that he just don't give a fuck. Little did he know he just opened up a door his ass can't close. "So, Envy what do you want to do?", she asked? "Well, I got him to agree to meet me at momma house so we can talk. I figure we strike then", I told her. "So, you think he's really going to come alone sis", she asked? "No, I really don't know or think he will really be alone", I said. "Honestly, I don't believe he will be alone but he definitely will play it that way. So, we are going to have to be prepared just in case he is on what we on sis", I told her. "I got a plan, just give me about an hour and I can put it in motion", Loyalty said.

We both ordered our food and just talked till it came. "Man Envy all this shit crazy". "Momma really was the shit huh sis", I smiled. "Yea she was just so damn beautiful", I continued. "Especially Joel popping up from the dead", I said. "Now that shit crazy sis for real how dare he just pop up now", I told Loyalty. "Well sis at least we still have one parent and he definitely wants to be here for us now. So, let's give him a chance", she told me. "I think we need a DNA test Loyalty. What if it's a set up to get our guard down. I mean we have to think about this all the way. QC is trying to take us out by any means, hell he is working with the woman who killed mona. Who's to say this Cuban man is not trying to help take us out", I explained. "Envy I'm not saying you're wrong but if he wanted to kill us, he could have so many times. Especially with all the pictures he has of us. He had way too many opportunities to do our asses. I think he's legit but if taking a DNA test will satisfy you, I'm with it", Loyalty said. Once we were done eating, I headed and grabbed a room to get changed to meet with QC later. I also needed some heat so I snuck to the spot I had low key and strapped up.

After leaving the restaurant with Envy I went and made a few moves. I called Joel and told him we needed about five good shooters. I also explained to him what we had up. He told me that he would meet us there and he was war ready. Just for the sake of Envy maybe I called up CoCo to round up her crew. I told her if she helped me with this the payout would be good, as well as compensation for any lost soldiers. Telling her to focus on everyone and if anyone looks against us to take their ass out. She told me to pull up and she had some shit for us. I headed to the park to meet the guy she had been waiting for. When I got there, he put a duffle bag in my backseat. He instructed me to call Coco once I looked inside as soon as possible. Once he was gone, I pulled off heading to Joel's house. It was time to let this muthafuckah QC pay.

I met back up with Envy at Joel's house, before she headed to mommy's house. She gave me a few guns and a vest. Joel also had us loaded with guns. He told us that he went and placed them all around momma's house. "So, you're the one who has been going into momma's house", I asked? "Yes, it was me. I have money stashed there. Just in case something happened to me y'all would eventually find it", he answered. While Envy loaded up her guns, I went and sat next to our father. "Are you ready, Loyalty", he grabbed my hand. Before I could even say a word. Envy walked into the room. "She's as ready as we're ever going to be. Question is "are you ready", she interrupted us. I then cocked my gus as I stood up. "Come on let's see if this muthafukah is ready for us.

`To Be Continued....

About the Author

JeDonna Mathis is an Author from Grand Rapids Michigan. She is thirty-two years old with a nine-year-old daughter, who enjoys writing as well. JeDonna started writing when she was a little girl. Always creating stories. Growing up JeDonna always wanted to become a writer and movie producer. As time continued JeDonna used writing as an escape from things happening around her.

Writing poetry, and short stories a lot. Passing her notebook around to peers and sharing her stories with everyone. JeDonna fell in love with Urban Fiction when she first read "The Coldest Winter Ever" in her early teenage years. When she was 17 years old JeDonna decided to write her own book. Within a year she had written two full books. Writing then became more than just a hobby for her, it became her passion. She still thought she wasn't ready for the world to read her work so she would only tell her friends about her books. One day JeDonna decided to allow her books to be seen by others. She then joined a publishing company and became a published author. Not knowing much and just being happy to accomplish something so big. She is the author of "When The Tables Turn", and "The Streets Loves No One" It's now 2022 and after dealing with two different publishers and going through so much.

JeDonna decided it was time she stepped out on faith and became an independent author. It was time to become self-published. JeDonna is now pushing full force to allow her books to reach hands around the world. Aiming towards big screens as well! JeDonna writes Urban Fiction, Erotica, Short Stories, and Children's books. She is super excited to publish under her own name and to learn so much. She thanks her Life Coach Matthew Santana Jr so much for believing in her and helping her as she faces a new journey of greatness to come!

Special Thanks

First and foremost I would like to thank God, for the gift to write. Blessing me with such a wide imagination. I want to thank all my family and friends who truly support my dreams. Most importantly I want to thank all my readers. None of this would be a reality without you. Thank you so much to my biggest inspiration, my daughter ZaMyah. She is my biggest fan. Thank you so much to Matthew Santana Jr with Santana Global Publications, for reaching out to me. Taking the time to help me with self-publishing this book. I really appreciate working with you and looking forward to many more projects in the future.

Special Thanks

First and foremost I would like to thank God, for the gift to write. Blessing me with such a wide imagination. I want to thank all my family and friends who truly support my dreams. Most importantly I want to thank all my readers. None of this would be a reality without you. Thank you so much to my biggest inspiration, my daughter ZaMyah. She is my biggest fan. Thank you so much to Matthew Santana Jr with Santana Global Publications, for reaching out to me. Taking the time to help me with self-publishing this book. I really appreciate working with you and looking forward to many more projects in the future.

Made in the USA
Middletown, DE
13 July 2024